THE PUPPETEER

a novel

Robert Kroetsch

Vintage Books • A Division of Random House • Toronto

First Vintage Edition, September 1993

Originally published in hardcover in Canada by Random House of Canada Limited, Toronto.

Canadian Cataloguing in Publication Data

Kroetsch, Robert, 1927–
The puppeteer

ISBN 0-394-22364-0

I. Title.

PS8521.R637P86 1993 C813'.54 C93-093843-7
PR9199.3.K76P86 1993

Cover design: Counterpunch/Linda Gustafson

Printed and bound in the United States

10 9 8 7 6 5 4 3 2 1

The Puppeteer

For the Willow Island gang.

1

The pizza man. That was her first name for him.

What made him look so silly at first, there on the porch with the rain behind him, was his hat. His tall black hat with its straight sides and its flat top, that and his unruly reddish-grey beard, made him look like nothing so much as a Greek Orthodox priest. He stepped back from the doorway, almost right off the porch, into the rain.

The Vancouver night was dense with a rain that was more a cold drizzle than a rain. Maggie tried to keep from smiling at the pizza man's near disaster, and perhaps that kept her from seeing the rest of his outfit. She found a purse under her left arm; she flattened some dollar bills and traded them for the cardboard box. She was thanking the pizza man, trying at once to give him a tip and to push shut the door, when she saw he had on not only the hat and beard of a priest or monk or whatever, but also a rain-splotched blue cassock. Or a shapeless blue sack of a garment that might pass for a cassock.

Perhaps he was just as startled as she. She was wearing a wedding dress. She had just that day discovered that when she put on her old wedding dress she could hear the story she intended to tell. She'd had no time to conceal the dress, rushing down the two flights of stairs from the attic to the front door.

The pizza man's look of surprise did not register with her until he had already turned away and was going down the porch steps, into the rain and the darkness. She switched off the porch light, then switched it on again. Four ivory-headed brass buttons stared in a row from a brass plate, but only two of them seemed connected to anything. She locked the door and looked out through the thick squares of distorting glass.

Maggie Wilder was new to her rented house, new at the age of forty-four to living alone. Her newly rented house was an old house; the February rains made it older, mouldier, smellier. The house stank. All of Vancouver stank of rain.

The pizza box was warm and reassuring. She carried it through the hallway and into the kitchen, then went to the fridge for a beer. She sat down at the large old kitchen table with the pizza, the beer, an opener, a stack of paper napkins. It was after midnight. The kitchen was warm and bright against the chill of the night and the endless splash and gurgle of rain. She couldn't get out of her mind the figure of the pizza man, awkward, looming there on her porch, yet for all his outlandish costume, somehow familiar and at home.

Her cousin's house was more borrowed than rented. George was her closest tie to Vancouver. He was a first cousin on her mother's side, and only fourteen hours her junior. In a way, they'd grown up twins. But, trust George, he'd up and left for the Far East one week before her return from the States. She hadn't expected that. The spiders moved into the house ahead of her. Only the kitchen was bright and decent, against the treacherous cold of the rain, against the pantry surprise of spiders, the sidewalk surprise of slugs the size of brown sausages. The kitchen was a cave of light hung with four calendars that didn't agree on the month or the year, as if George, when he was troubled, simply abandoned one point in time and moved to another.

Maggie lit a cigarette to go with the pizza and the beer and the watery silence of the old house. She took one deep drag on the cigarette, then stubbed it out on a soggy spot on the lid of the pizza box. She'd made a vow to Henry that she'd stop smoking. She'd left him to go away for a year, to be free of him — that was the agreement — and yet at the same time she'd made him that promise.

She was stubbing out the cigarette and absent-mindedly staring at the almost invisible colours in the skirt of her wedding dress when she noticed for the first time, in the intricate embroidery and beadwork on her lap, the outline in miniature of the dress she was wearing. The dressmaker who had filled the dress with detail had, with the same care, left blank an outline of the dress no larger than a postage stamp.

Maggie had seen, somewhere before, the face of the pizza man. She forced herself out of the wooden chair and went into the hallway and turned and climbed the broad and carpeted stairway to the second floor. She hurried along the hallway, pausing to straighten an oriental runner. She opened the door that led to the narrow attic stairway, looked up into the dark stairwell, switched on a light, tramped loudly up the bare wooden steps.

There was always someone waiting, even if it was only the version of herself that was supposed to be at work, writing the life she would have lived if she hadn't, in one reckless moment of caring too much or caring not at all, agreed to marry a man named Henry Ketch.

Perhaps it was her finding the dress, twenty-three years earlier, that made her agree to marry the man she had until then been refusing to marry. The dress wasn't merely white, it had been embroidered in pastel shades, and beadwork had been added, delicate and silvery. The dress was second hand when Maggie bought it and took it home and showed it to the graduate student in art history who was begging her to marry him and go back with him to Upstate New York.

The woman who sold the dress, in a little shop on a shabby street in Vancouver, had insisted on telling the bald truth. The dress had brought disaster to its first wearer. And Maggie had liked that too. She had liked the danger.

The desk was centred on an elaborate carpet in the middle of the rough wooden floor. Maggie went directly to the desk, not looking into the corners of the large attic. Her cousin George was a botanist; the spaces under the sloping walls were used to store boxes and crates and sacks that must contain botanic specimens. She hadn't so far had the courage to look.

In the attic, at her desk, she picked up a pen and tried to make notes on a blank pad. Damn her husband and his Greek icons and his trips to find more Greek icons. He always knew better, no matter what she said about people. He'd glance quickly through one of the few short stories she ever managed to complete, and then he'd say, well, yes, I suppose some people *might* get carried away like that, they might behave that recklessly. But now he was in Greece and their house on the Susquehanna River was rented to strangers.

She had seen the pizza man somewhere before. She tried to recollect. She saw in her mind a bearded man. Or perhaps he wasn't bearded. But his eyes were unchanged.

Stop it, she told herself, you're losing it again. Do something. Talk to someone.

She put down her pen without writing a word. The desk was heavy, oaken, just a shade too high. She stood up from the desk and the typewriter and turned and went down the steep stairway. She stopped on the second floor and went into her bedroom. She changed from the dress into a sweater and slacks and went down the second flight of stairs. The only phone in the house was in the kitchen.

The Japanese print on the calendar beside the fridge was by Utamaro. In the upper left-hand corner a man read a love letter while behind him his mistress, raising a mirror to cast more light, tried to read over his shoulder, while under the verandah a spy read the trailing end of the long letter.

Maggie hated the rain. She came very close to hating the house.

She glanced now at the calendar that hung over the ironing board that for three days, a week, whatever, she hadn't bothered to put away. Two Inuit shamans drew objects out of or hurled them into the air, she couldn't decide which. She let her gaze go blank on the Texaco calendar with its winter season that was, at least at first glance, mostly snow falling on snow. She read again the blue and commercial elegance of the Royal Bank calendar with its pictureless design, some of its dates scribbled over, made illegible by whatever it was that George did or expected to do or, Maggie suspected, neglected to do. She had become an expert on those calendars, while in the attic study two floors up her typewriter and the spiders conspired in the oozing dark, and outside the loud silence waited in the maudlin rain.

She made a careful note of the hour on the Japanese calendar. That enigmatic detail, printed boldly in red, would help the police discover who murdered her. It was 1:22 in the morning, February 14, at least by that calendar, when she phoned Midnight Pizza and asked for a second delivery.

The woman with the old and authoritative voice who answered the phone was at once inquisitive and not at all surprised when Maggie asked that the mushroom and black olive pizza be delivered by the man in the blue or bluish dress-like affair —

"I know, I know," the woman said over the phone, interrupting the rehearsed description. "Papa Vasilis. Papa B. You want him to make the delivery."

It was not quite too late to turn back. Maggie knew that. She had an instant in which she could fail to give a name and an address.

The old-sounding woman sighed an audacious sigh. "I'll see if he's still working. Sometimes he goes out to make a delivery and forgets to come back. God only knows where he gets to —"

Maggie hung up the receiver as if in danger of breaking the phone from the wall. She could, she assured herself, still call back and cancel the order.

She had time. She knew that. She knew, almost to the minute, when a pizza would come out of the oven at Midnight Pizza, how long it would take a driver to get to her door.

She delayed or avoided a decision or both by wondering what the police would say if she phoned and asked about the imposter who went around dressed as a Greek monk, delivering pizza. They would caution her, she decided. He is, in his bizarre fashion, almost attractive, she would say, feigning mild curiosity. He's a harmless eccentric, they would say, but if you feel uneasy —

He didn't show up at all, in the time she knew it should take. Relief and disappointment followed her around the kitchen as she tried to make lists. She must do some serious shopping, start to cook seriously for herself. George had a whole row of cookbooks. His telephone book was shabby and out of date, but she must try to remember the names of old acquaintances. The trouble was, first names and last names and vaguely remembered addresses didn't match up in the book that had grown hugely during her years of absence. First names had become initials. Last names had changed or attached themselves by hyphens to other names.

She was on her way to find her only pack of Camels, hidden behind a row of cookbooks, when the doorbell rang. She checked the grandfather clock in the hallway before unlocking the door: 2:18 in the morning.

He stood like a magician in front of the curtain of rain. She saw, to her surprise and somewhat to her relief, that he was a man in his late forties. She'd guessed the first time she saw him that he was younger, closer to her husband's age. He looked as if, instead of trying to keep dry, he'd made every effort to get soggy wet.

Papa B offered her the pizza box.

"Come in out of the rain," she said. She left him holding the pizza. "I'll just get my purse."

She had meant to say, just hang on while I catch up with myself. He was inside the door, clumsy, awkward, holding on to the box he was trying to deliver. She had left her purse on a chair that was pushed against the kitchen table.

Hurrying toward the kitchen, she knew he was behind her. She was saying something about coffee. That had not been her intention. She'd considered the idea and rejected it. Not so much as a cup of coffee. They would be strangers pretending at courtesies. Instead, now, they were acting like two lovers, attempting to recover something by pretending to be strangers. And that had been one of her fantasies too. But not with this man. She'd thought of trying to return to Henry that way, she and Henry risking small insinuations, almost reaching out.

Maggie, while starting to make coffee, managed to see how Papa B's face, in some failed way, was long and ascetic. His hazel eyes seemed lost in the serious contemplation of nothing. His nose was strong and might have been, accidentally, left out in the rain by its face. His curly and darkish hair was streaked grey, his beard was grey and red. He glanced around as if counting the calendars. She noticed then the small bun of hair at the back of his head.

"Broadway Bakery and Pastry," Papa B said.

Maggie glanced up from where she was setting water to boil on the stove. Papa B nodded toward the plastic bag and its croissants on the counter. "My favourite bakery."

Murderers and fugitives weren't supposed to have favourite bakeries. Why didn't he get on with it, whip out a knife from under his cassock? The waiting was brutal. Like having a loaded gun for company. "It's fresh. Want a croissant with your coffee?"

"Just don't offer me pizza." He smiled a guarded smile.

Maggie laughed. "I sort of guessed that."

"Coffee will do the trick. I just saw a friend, a man who can't sleep. Ever, he claims. Not ever. He doesn't serve much coffee."

"Papa B," she said. She had to test that name on him, push it against his concealed sense of who he was. She was alone with a stranger whose face seemed a familiar one, and only that obnoxious woman who took the pizza order knew about the rendezvous. "Papa Vasilis," Maggie added.

She waited to hear a gap between her naming and the man himself.

"This last delivery was tacked on to my list. Your special request."

He too waited. He noticed that his hat was dripping water onto the table and he reached and lifted the hat and wiped at the water with the loose, ragged sleeve of his cassock. He looked weary beyond the bones of his body. He was talking about a friend who didn't sleep, who might not ever know something so mundane and welcome as sleep.

"You have no accent," Maggie said. "You seem —"

"I was born here. My parents went back to Greece — they took me back when I was a kid."

Maggie in that instant wanted to believe him. She was tempted to believe his patient, explaining voice, his answer to a question he'd heard ten, a dozen, fifty times. No, I am not a foreigner, but I am a foreigner, yes.

"And you," he said. "When did you come back?"

Maggie, trying to open the coffee tin, froze. She glanced quickly at his bright, even teeth, under the reddish-grey moustache that needed trimming, then back to the tin of coffee in her left hand. She had somehow to get the plastic lid off the tin, then measure out coffee, then pour hot water into the funnel of white paper without scalding herself to death.

"You're Maggie Wilder, aren't you?"

She was dumbfounded. And yet she was not without her instant of elation. Perhaps she had come back for this, to be recognized, heralded, after all the years of obscurity, even if it cost her her life, goddamnit.

"Bludgett," Papa B said. "My insomniac friend. He's a lawyer. He's always reading."

"Legal cases, I trust." She hoped her voice offered just a hint of spite. Murder cases, she wanted to add. Stories about murderers who disappeared and then had to be traced through all their disguises and then properly tried and then properly exposed and then properly imprisoned and tortured and hanged.

"Not just legal stuff. He reads everything, even your work."

She felt the rise and swoop of her heart. "I've only written one book in my whole life. One small book."

"I just took him a pizza. You gave your name as Maggie Wilder when you ordered your second pizza." Papa B's hands moved widely in the air, not so much attached to as separated from his mere body by the baggy sleeves. "Different from the first time. I guess it was the dress you had on. When you called in the second order I couldn't help but remember."

"You told the story to your friend?" Her tone was at once a reprimand and a request for clarification.

"He's always reading," Papa B said. "Like his life depends on it. He says you wrote a book of stories that are mostly set in Greece."

She gave him a chance to go on. She passed him a knife and two plates and wanted him to explain, to add with a pleased smile, he likes your stories, he thinks you hit it right on the head, the stupid things people do that change their whole lives —

"You must have been there — according to Bludgett's guess — maybe five years ago."

"Four." She took down two cups from the open cupboard shelves and checked with a finger inside each. George's cups had a way of coming off the shelf dusty and stained. Out in the hallway the grandfather clock ticked so slowly she could, easily, between the ticks, scream for help. "It will be four years this coming fall."

"I was there — stayed three years. Then I took a notion to come back." Papa B seemed with an enormous heave of his body to change the subject.

She wanted to say, you're forgetting that you just told me you went there as a child.

"Two pizzas in one night." He looked around the kitchen. "Lucky for you you don't have to watch your weight."

He was without imagination. He was as blank as his face.

But then she thought, he's testing me. He wants to know who else lives in the house. But she was angry too, yes, she was putting on weight, damnit. Seventeen days since her return and she hadn't been able to pick a name from the phone book, let alone dial. She hadn't looked for a single old acquaintance, not for a friend from university, not for a childhood friend. Because, she knew, it was not the past she was looking for, it was something else. A turn she had missed. A single minute the clock of her life had skipped, breaking the sequence, leaving her marooned in a time of her own.

She should tell him, there are two kids upstairs, asleep, they ate the first pizza. That made her think of her two sons, grown up, gone from the home they'd grown up in. They'd fled early, the way she was fleeing now, late.

She too knew how to change the subject. "So," she said, "instead of overeating I should consult a monk who looks as if he's trying to win a prize for starving. Trying to win sainthood —"

"I'm hardly a monk." Papa B, tearing the cardboard, ignoring the croissants on the counter, opened the pizza box. He picked up the knife and freed two slices of pizza and set one each on a plate. He was gone, again, from the conversation. "So Bludgett was right about the monicker," he said, addressing himself.

Maggie sagged. She didn't quite have the strength to attempt an evasion. "My husband's name is Ketch. Henry Ketch. I'm Maggie Wilder because I decided not to take his name. But sometimes I hide behind it. That bothers him."

Perhaps she was assuring her guest, there is a husband upstairs, half asleep, watching television, a huge man with a jealous disposition and a violent temper. Except that Henry was a smallish man with not a streak of jealousy in him, and he was somewhere on Mount Athos again, as usual, as always, looking for still more icons to look at because he was, endlessly, writing a study of the idea of time in Greek iconographic painting.

"My husband's work takes him to Greece. I go there with him, fairly often." She was tempted to correct what she had just said: I used to go there fairly often. I'll never go there again.

"I was —" Papa B went on chewing — "over a period of years — a worker — in a monastery there in Greece — the monks — gave me these discards —"

Maggie thinking: disguise. Gave you that disguise. In order to get rid of who you really were. You might at least pretend. Or is that part of your disguise, letting us think we see right through you?

"Don't tell me," she said. "Mount Athos. You were on Mount Athos. That place where they don't allow females. Not even female animals. No mares or milk cows or female donkeys, no chickens that lay eggs. Henry's little litany."

Papa B nodded. He was deaf, the man, to any kind of snooping. He was a walking, deliberate blank space.

"My husband's been there five times. To your precious Mount Athos. To study icons. He's there now. Or on his way."

Why did she dare to tell him that? She held her breath in order to hold her tongue. She wanted to go on explaining. Henry and his Guggenheim, we're separated now, a trial separation. Our house rented for a year to a visiting professor. I can't go back. Our two sons, finally, away at college. I won't go back. Henry couldn't understand. Then I told him, I said, I'm going there to write the autobiography of a wedding dress.

"You see," she said, "he claims he's found the icons of his life this time. He keeps phoning. Telling me where he can be reached." She shook her head. "So I can surprise him and show up and look after him."

There were black spots of something or other in George's sugar bowl, along with caked sugar. It seemed to be the sugar bowl that made Papa B put down his slice of pizza and pick up his hat. "I must be off. Sorry. I'm sorry."

Just that suddenly he was not so much the returned man as the fugitive. He was up and running. He must scurry back to one of his hiding places.

"The coffee is ready." Maggie indicated the mess she'd made on the counter beside the stove, the coffee she'd thought about and forgotten and was reminded of now.

"You'd like my friend." Papa B nodded wearily, all the while guessing at where his head might be and trying to put on his hat. "Come and meet him."

"I couldn't possibly. I have work to do."

"Tomorrow. Tomorrow night." He glanced at the clock on the stove. "Tonight, I mean. This coming midnight.

I'd take you to meet him now, but my lady is expecting me."

Now where in hell did he get that language? My *lady*. Maggie wanted him to trip on the skirt of his cassock as he turned away. Go see your *lady*.

He was in the hallway, reaching for the doorknob. He stretched his left arm out of its sleeve and glanced at his wrist as if looking at a watch. There was no watch on his wrist.

"I'll be here at midnight sharp. Right on the button."

He was gone through the door. He left the door open and Maggie was alone with the rattle of his boots on the steps of the porch, with the steady sound of the rain.

2

Maggie Wilder is writing this. Reading over her left shoulder, I become a loving supporter, the champion of her need to get the story of her wedding dress down on paper. Now and then I say a few words, joining myself into her train of thought. Sometimes, perhaps just to tease me, she scrambles a few of my words in amongst her own.

I'm much too old and gone in the eyes to do her sort of work. Being a collector does that for the eyes. I had been looking high and low for her pizza man, but all to no avail, all to much anguish. Then this Maggie Wilder sat like a dozing cat and the mouse came to her paw.

She hardly slept at all, after his second departure. Then at dawn she fell into a dreamless sleep. Then at noon she awoke to a splitting headache.

By mid-afternoon the rain was a charge of dynamite, deep under water. The birds swam in exploding air. Maggie, under her green umbrella, walked north to West Broadway, then east toward Midnight Pizza. She liked, that fateful day, the Vancouver rain — and the way it cloaked her intention. The gusting wind carried the rain in under the umbrella, straight at the tension around her blue eyes. And she does have careful eyes, eyes that miss nothing.

She wouldn't, she resolved, at every red light, at the door of the restaurant itself, allow herself to stop for coffee. She would leave a message for Papa B. She coaxed the message into her mind. Sorry, the message said. Can't make it. Personal matters.

She liked the pun, even as it surprised her. Personal matters. She followed her open umbrella through the door, trying the message on the cold wetness of the rain that kissed the edges of her mouth.

And he was there.

He was as real as mud. Papa B, his back to the door, his hat on the table beside his right elbow, the bun of hair at the back of his neck conspicuous and absurd, was the only customer at Midnight Pizza. And he wasn't a customer.

A youngish waitress, absent-minded and intense, moved through the symmetry of tables and chairs and lattice-framed booths, wiping at the red plastic ketchup containers. Maggie, ignored, waited. She came close to liking the place, with its wall paintings of classical sites, the Parthenon, the Colosseum, Pompeii, Delphi, Hadrian's Villa. You name it. Large paintings executed recklessly in aggressive, tumbling shapes and teasing pastels.

The phone rang just as Maggie closed her umbrella.

The waitress, turning reluctantly toward the sound, acknowledged Maggie, pointed her to a table, then fumbled her way toward the phone as if she had never before made the journey.

"No," the waitress said. She paused. "Yes, this is Elizabeth, who did you expect, Mae West? Ida won't be here for another ten minutes. You know that, Josie. Why do you phone me every day just ten minutes before she gets here? You know she's always exactly ten minutes late for work."

Papa B at his table raised his head and turned around as if about to call a message across the room. But he spoke to Maggie, not to Elizabeth. "You're early. Good."

The presumption in his voice, the error, offended Maggie. "What do you mean, I'm early, good?"

"I've been waiting. This time the coffee is on me."

But Elizabeth interrupted. She refused to serve coffee either to him or to Maggie. "That order is up. For that lawyer friend of yours, the tax swindler. You can have your coffee after."

Maggie was about to be left high and dry. She had come to tell Papa B she wouldn't go with him to meet Bludgett and now Papa B was mumbling through his last swallow of coffee, attaching his hat to his head, signalling her to hurry.

"Chinatown." He pointed as if Chinatown must be somewhere in the room. "Time you got out of that house you're hiding in."

"The Prynn order is ready," Elizabeth said. "You can drop it on your way."

And so they drove in the daytime streets of Vancouver, Maggie and Papa B. At first they did not speak at all. They drove in the pelting rain, on the rain-slick streets, Papa B with his tall black hat beside him, Maggie next to the hat, the two orders stacked in insulator bags on the back seat.

South they drove, from Broadway, down along Dunbar, into the Kerrisdale streets where Maggie grew into childhood. It was rush-hour time, loud, dizzying. Stong's Supermarket was there. The fish and chips parlour was gone. The Blue Moon was gone, with its candy and gum, a bookstore in its place. Second-hand books. Copies of her own slim volume, perhaps. She wanted to stop and look, a table outside the door, books under a plastic sheet.

"Turn here, would you?" she said.

Papa B, silent, obeyed.

They were on 36th. Moving slowly. To where the house of her dead parents must still stand, next to a potato patch. Rows of potatoes then, the green rows in furious white blossom. She recognized the house, hiding behind a blister of shrubs. The potato patch had sprouted a bungalow. And the peach tree wasn't there, the tree she slid down one night to go meet a boy in the nearby forest. But the boy didn't show, that night, in the dark. The tree was gone now.

Papa B drove to the end of the street, where the forest loomed in the rain. He made a left turn, another left turn. He stopped.

Papa B was gone, with a pizza. Maggie reached to the radio. She wanted him back in the car, protecting her, protecting her child's world. He would never return. She had walked through the potato patch with her father on one side of a row of potatoes, she on the other; they swung each a scrap of shingle, knocking potato bugs into their pails. It took forever.

A car pulled close behind. Then stopped.

Maggie turned down her window and put out an arm to signal the driver by. The windows had begun to fog over, she couldn't see clearly. She was convinced, with piercing certainty, that the driver behind her was a cop. She reached and pressed the horn.

The car behind pulled out, passed, drove on. Papa B came running down the steps from the small bungalow.

"What did you do, stop for pizza?" Maggie held a hand to her thumping heart.

"The Prynn kid there — her mother's a hooker. I deliver pizza and look in to see that her daughter's okay."

"At this hour?"

He missed her question. "It's this time of day that scares the kid." He reached to turn up the defroster. "Just home from school. The house empty. Some kids hate empty houses."

But Maggie's sons were gone from home, gone and happy to be gone, in college and liking it, planning careers as secure as their father's career, the father they insisted they didn't like.

Papa B said nothing more and Maggie was impatient. She was offended at his nonchalance, at his simple impulse to be a good man. It was his city, he was looking after it, there was nothing else to be said or done, get on with the job. The pious fraud. He believed in his own disguise, even if it didn't for an instant fool another human being. He would deliver food to the hungry and throw in consolation to boot. And all the while he didn't have the bare courtesy to ask why she was collapsing right there in the wet afternoon, having a nervous breakdown.

She would be as stubbornly silent as he. They swung onto Dunbar. She turned the radio silent and sat silent herself, remembering the streetcar rides from 41st up Dunbar to go to Broadway for ice cream at Peter's. The exactness of ice cream. Vanilla is not chocolate. Names. Strawberry. Maple walnut. Words. Peter's, where she and her friends sat at the large windows facing the street and drank milkshakes out of tall glasses, poured again from the shiny metal containers, filled their glasses again, and still had more milkshake to drink.

Flying west, she had written down the names of streets. She had listed the streets, remembering porches, bicycles dropped on sidewalks, open garage doors, parked cars, conversations. She wrote the names of the streets inside the back cover of a Victorian novel she'd taken along to while away the time. Perhaps she'd left the novel on the plane, she'd had one drink more than she'd needed. In her eighteen days of delay, if it was delay, she hadn't opened the phone book to anything but the nearest pizza place.

"That Prynn kid," Papa B said. "She sits there and plays the piano. My father did that. When he was supposed to be out putting up hay or branding calves."

"You —" She had somehow imagined he existed in a solitariness so vast it excluded ancestors and progeny alike. She dared to remember her own father, a logger, usually out in the forest, seldom at home. Or when he came home, he was still out in the forest.

"I'm divorced," Papa B said. He gestured out past the windshield wipers. "That was a long time ago," he added. He spoke as if his past had fallen away like useless dead branches from a tree.

"In this city?"

"Long ago and far away. I'm like you."

She resented the comparison. She loathed it. "I'm not divorced. I have a husband and two sons. We write and we call." She was embarrassed at the claim. Two letters to each son in the eighteen days since her departure. And she hadn't phoned at all, she couldn't trust herself with the concern that would speak in their voices. Henry did all the phoning. She had to show him. He'd said he would find an island when he left Mount Athos. He had an island picked out. He'd rent a place with an extra bedroom that would serve as a study where she could sit and pretend to write her autobiography of a dress. And they had argued about that too, that had been the subject of their parting words. "Biography," Henry said, correcting her. "Autobiography," Maggie said. And then she was going through security.

Papa B swerved to avoid a jogger. He stopped the car at a stoplight and a police car pulled up on their left. The cop in the passenger's seat turned down his window and stared at Papa B. Or at Maggie. Perhaps he recognized her, she thought in a moment of panic, perhaps he was thinking, I went to school with that woman, what crazy stunt is she up to now?

"That prick," Papa B said. "That particular cop. He does this to me."

Maggie wanted to jump out of the car and make a run for it, into the rain. Or she could reach across Papa B, turn down his window, shout, What's the crime I'm accessory to?

The light turned green. Both cars seemed stalled, fixed in motionless solitude under the pelting rain. And then the police car leapt forward.

Suddenly, for Maggie, the city was beautiful, in the shine of rain. She had escaped from a trap or a destiny. Papa B nodded in response to her retrieved glance and they moved into an exquisite right turn. They burst out of light, into a tree-black street. They moved slowly through varieties of dark, generously downward.

"Shortcut." That was all Papa B said.

They coasted through a stutter of breaking and reilluminating light. The car stopped at a beautiful, shining stop sign, then flowed like water itself into a new and anonymous and engulfing stream of traffic.

Perhaps he wasn't frightened at all, just irked. She breathed deeply. He was confident, street smart. He was hiding, brilliantly, by driving in conspicuous disguise through the patrolled streets. The escape thrilled her. She was shamelessly proud of this anonymous friend. All around, the store fronts flashed golden and red and a lambent white with their treasuries of mysterious signs and extravagant invitations. The unspeaking mannequins turned their heads to smile. Elegant sofas, dressed in flowers and silver thread, bellied against the plate-glass windows. Doorways split like ripe fruit to spill the promise of secret and gorgeous lives. Rain fell onto the city like an infinitely large flock of infinitely small birds.

"He lives in Chinatown," Papa B said. "Did I tell you that?"

"I think you told me that."

"He lives two floors up in a building that should have been torn down years ago."

"He won't mind our showing up this way?"

"I warned him earlier."

"But I didn't really say I'd join you."

"He said you'd show." Papa B pointed over his right shoulder with his left hand. "He likes pizza the way you do."

"It's not that I like pizza. I've been cooking for twenty-odd years — without two days off in a row."

"One of the things I like about you is, you never exaggerate." Papa B had found a parking space. "He's looking forward to seeing you."

Maggie followed after Papa B. They were climbing stairs — one flight, then another. The stairway was dirty, badly lit. Before Papa B could knock, the door at the head of the stairs opened.

Thomas Bludgett was holding a book. He hardly glanced up during introductions. He was looking at the back of the book rather than at Maggie when he said, "You don't look like your picture." He showed her the back of the book, daring her to contradict him.

Maggie saw on the jacket of the book a photograph of herself with bangs that she didn't recall ever having, an ambiguous set to her mouth that said, I'm dangerous, I'm afraid, I take chances, I don't take chances, love me. The eyes of the photograph glared blanky into Maggie's own.

"*Trading Places,*" Bludgett read from the book's spine. He didn't open the book or look at its cover. "You seem to know Greece inside out."

"I knew it from inside — from the inside of small rooms in cheap hotels. I got to know the rooms and my two children very well while my husband was out looking at icons. I thought I made that clear in the stories. I didn't know anything about Greece. That was the point."

Bludgett was wearing a red flannel shirt that hadn't been ironed. He had a slept-in-his-clothes look, for a man who was supposed to be insomniac.

"On the last page of the last story there's a woman who remembers her wedding dress. She says that one day she is going to put it on again. See what happens."

"That has nothing to do with pizza."

"Maybe. Maybe not."

"You and my husband would get along fine."

Bludgett moved the tea kettle off the stove, then turned and carried away his copy of Maggie's book, disappearing through a doorway made narrow by stacked books and a protruding bookcase. Maggie watched his disappearance. His hair was unruly and dark and in need of trimming. He was a little over forty and still at that age pretending to look older than he really was, as if afraid the bouncer in some favourite bar might unexpectedly check his ID and throw him out.

"Here it is. I've found it." Bludgett was speaking in the next room, either to Maggie or to the photograph on the back of the book. "Listen. 'The catalogue of human errors begins with the hands. The catalogue was written on the dress that she put into storage on the afternoon of their wedding day. She wanted to take the dress out of its sealed —' "

"I'd forgotten that. I swear I had."

"Good try."

Bludgett was in the doorway again, manipulating his tall, evasive figure into the kitchen. He had not, after all, put the book away. He closed it and put it front cover down on the crowded table and reached to move the kettle, almost scalding himself. Maggie liked the way he had of trying to step around his own presence. He was wearing Indian moccasin slippers decorated with beadwork in geometrical designs. She liked the way his jeans fit.

"If dresses could talk," Maggie said.

Bludgett was measuring tea leaves with a wooden spoon into a Chinese teapot. "Josie Pavich — I talked to her this morning." He glanced at Papa B, then at the teapot again. "She made the dress. She remembers the dress, but she says she doesn't remember you. Brides look alike, she says — in the long run, it's the dresses that differ."

"You sound like a man who has never been married."

"Unlucky in love." Bludgett nodded agreement to himself. "Josie makes wedding dresses for a living. It's kept her single all her life."

"And you?"

"I used to practise law."

Maggie spoke to the picture of herself on her book. "The woman who sold me the dress warned me. She'd had it back in her shop for a week. She was selling it, she said, so the man who returned it could never change his mind."

"He has changed his mind," Bludgett said. "He wants the dress."

"And the bride? Did she change her mind too?"

"She went over a cliff in a car," Bludgett said.

"You never quite give answers."

"She's dead."

"I'm sorry."

"Forget it." Bludgett was moving books off a chair so he too could sit at the table. "I mean, forget it, get it out of your mind, go back to writing what you call fiction. You were safer doing that."

"I'm a little bit on the stubborn side. You can see that in the photograph" — she was pointing — "even if it doesn't look like me."

"How do you like your tea?" Bludgett said.

Papa B, his elbows on the pizza box, was sipping at the lip of a small, empty, elegant, reddish-brown porcelain bowl. "In its own way that dress — it might just be talking. Don't you think?"

He was often a few sentences behind in a conversation.

Papa B went on with the conversation he had initiated with himself. "Jack Deemer. He wants the dress for the same reason that he wants me. He wants, so to speak, to keep us quiet."

3

As you have no doubt guessed, I am Papa B's Jack Deemer. And Maggie's precious Papa B had, for a change, got something right. I wanted him quiet and just a bit more. I made no bones about that to anyone, ever. I wanted him stone-cold dead. I confess as much right here and now. Let's get that out of the way. And let's skip the business of attaching blame.

Why Julie Magnuson married me instead of the man she'd intended to marry when she ordered her wedding dress is something we'll touch on later, if it promises to shed any light. At any rate, Julie and I, after the knot was tied, went rushing away from the altar to a room in a hotel. The was how it was done then, believe me.

The hotel was in a ramshackle wooden ghost town on the eastern slopes of the Rocky Mountains. When the coal mines closed down, the miners and the business people and their families had no choice but to move away. But they kept on returning — to hold a wake and to bury the corpse. Or to get married.

Julie and I got hitched in a ramshackle wooden church that was opened only for special events. The ghost town's one hotel, on the other hand, had managed to stay in business. Hunters in the fall. Fishermen. Campers in need of a shower and a night without mosquitoes. And then of course there were always the crowds of former residents who showed up for the funerals and the weddings.

Julie and I, before the candles were snuffed, were in our room and undressing. And then, two hours later, I made what was, granted, a silly mistake. I returned the wedding dress to the woman who had done the sewing and the beadwork and the embroidery.

"It's *whose* dress?" Maggie Wilder said, in reply to Bludgett's evasive and cautionary remarks. He had given her the warning but not the story. "You're going to tell me it isn't *my* dress? Well just you try to get your hands on it."

But for two days she couldn't touch it herself. She couldn't bring herself to put the dress back on. Bludgett, with all his care and incompetence, had tumbled her deep into silence.

On the afternoon of the third day Maggie Wilder went again for coffee to Midnight Pizza. This time Elizabeth, the waitress, was not alone. Maggie sat down in a booth across the aisle from where two old women at a table were having coffee. Or, rather, she found herself directed by Elizabeth to that particular booth.

Elizabeth, turning a cup upright on its saucer in front of Maggie, looked directly into Maggie's face. "Some hair of the dog. That's what you need. Not coffee."

"Do I look that bad?"

"Worse. You look like something the cat drug in. You look like the Franklin Expedition."

Maggie opened a small plastic container of milk and waited while Elizabeth poured. "And worse yet, I haven't been drinking."

The larger of the two old women at the table leaned across the aisle toward Maggie. "You can tell me. I once got polluted on lemon gin."

"And I cleaned up the toilet bowl," the other woman said.

The two old women laughed. Then the larger woman said to Maggie, "I recognized your voice. You must have eaten a bushel basket of pizzas by now." She was heavily built, big-boned. She let the thickness of her body give weight to her rough, gentle voice. "I'm Ida Babcock."

"I'm Maggie."

"I know. Papa B told us to keep an eye out for you." Ida pointed across the table at her friend. "This here is Josie."

"I'm Josie — Josie Pavich," Josie said, reassuring Maggie. She was a small, quick woman who suddenly found a handkerchief in a pocket of her sweater and just in the nick of time caught the drip at the tip of her nose. "It's the damned weather," she added. "Fog so thick this morning the rain couldn't fall."

"It's her sewing gives her asthma," Ida said, "not the weather. It's all that lint. We live down there in Asthma Flats, and that doesn't help either." She pointed accusingly at Josie. "When there are people stupid enough to get married, they go see Josie. And there are lots of them."

"Keeps me out of mischief." Josie was a petite, dodgy woman, her hair at once blonde and grey. "Ida was a cook. Until she got the arthritis in both her hands." With a quick motion Josie found again the handkerchief she'd pushed into a sleeve of her sweater. "We pay our way. Even if Papa B does drive us around in his pizza car like a pair of old crowbaits."

"While he's hunted like a mad dog," Ida added.

Maggie heard her chance in the stiff, angular air. She put down her cup and tried to find her mouth with her lips. Her elbows wanted to slide away from each other.

"He's my nephew," Ida went on, before Maggie spoke. "That's why he does it. Not because he feels sorry for a pair of old buzzards like us."

Then Maggie said, "He's a monk of some sort, I take it. From that outfit he wears."

Josie snorted. "Monk, my Royal American."

"In his own way," Ida said, defending her nephew, "he is what he is. And I'll tell you something else. I'll tell the plain truth, and I'll repeat it right in front of the chief of police, and the Pope along with him, if you can catch the Pope at home. Papa B is as innocent as the day is long."

Josie started to speak and was interrupted.

"The poor man has been hounded right out of his wits," Ida said, nodding. To Josie. To Maggie. "If it isn't the police who are after him it's the crook the police should be looking for when they're looking for Papa B instead. What's his name, Josie?"

"Mr Jack Deemer, thief and thug."

"There," Ida said. "Do you believe me?"

Maggie offered her right arm. "Here. Twist my rubber arm."

And if the two old women, a single moment earlier, had been little more than a pair of strangers, in the moment of Maggie's speaking they became her allies, friendly co-conspirators in a treacherous world. Even the waitress, Elizabeth, lolling against the counter by the phone and the cash register, was not entirely to be trusted.

"Papa B." Josie ducked her small body low, then slid her words like secrets across the table's shining surface. "He told us about you. We thought you'd never show up."

"Hounded," Ida said, retrieving the word that Josie had managed to lose track of. "And yet he's as innocent as a newborn lamb. And I'll tell you why." She squared her wide shoulders. "Are you listening?"

"I'm all ears."

"No one has ever produced a body. That's why. That's why he's innocent."

"Tell that to Mr Jack Deemer," Josie said.

"Jack Deemer, indeed." Ida opened her fists, stretching the fingers of her stiff hands. "Jack Deemer ought to be in the crowbar hotel."

"Or pushing up daisies," Josie said. "I couldn't agree more. But the trouble is, he didn't fire the gun. Your nephew fired the gun."

"He did, yes. He pulled the trigger. He said so himself." Maggie nodded her granting of that much. "He fired a shot at that little dwarf doctor who was dumb enough to be standing straight up in the stern end of a canoe." Briefly, she stuck out her tongue at no one in particular — "he missed."

Josie winced. "But he hit the canoe. Papa B hit the bow of that canoe when he fired the shot that he himself admitted he fired." She tried the voice of reason against her friend's unlikely proposition. "That dwarf was standing up in the stern of the canoe because he was so short he didn't have any choice, and when the canoe got hit, bingo, over the side he went."

"But where's the body?" Ida insisted. "The body did not come up —"

"Come up, indeed," Josie said. "No, the corpse did not come bobbing up like a scrub brush in a bucket." And maybe the corpse had some rocks in its pockets to help keep it down."

"They dragged," Ida said, countering with the authority of her larger voice. "They dragged the lake for a mile in every direction. They hired that diver that almost got drownded, tangled up down there in some steamboat wreck. But nothing and nobody ever came back with a body."

Josie's aggrieved tone acknowledged that she was losing ground. "That lake has no bottom. In a lot of places. Somebody should have fired a cannon."

Ida was pressing her victory. "When my husband died right there on our Alberta homestead in the middle of the night in the middle of a blizzard at least I had a body as evidence. And if I killed him, at least he died the way he claimed he wanted to die."

"You're always exaggerating," Josie said. "You have no respect for the truth."

"Don't truth me," Ida said. "I was there in that shack with the body for two days and two nights." She was claiming the spoils of her victory. "I couldn't get to the barn, through that blizzard, to harness a team of horses. Don't tell me —"

"Do you want me to get the phone?" Elizabeth called from where she was doing nothing. "Or are you planning to stagger to your feet today?"

"Kee-rist on a fishhook!" Ida hauled herself up from her chair and went to the counter and answered the phone, picking up her pencil while she spoke, preparing to write down an order. She paused, then frowned. She put down the pencil beside the order pad and clamped her freed hand on to the telephone receiver. Silently she shaped with her lips a word.

"Inez," Josie said to Maggie, whispering, translating the word that Ida mouthed. "Inez. She owns this place. And lots of other pizza places in this city. Our pizza king in this town is a lady. You watch how we jump if she shows up."

4

Maggie put on the wedding dress.

The large attic was long and narrow, with a stairway at one end that led up from a door on the second floor. The sloping wall at Maggie's back was broken by a dormer window. The wall at the opposite end from the stairwell had in it two windows and in one of the windows was a fan that let in rain and the sound of rain and the wail of the wind. Between the two windows ran the red brick chimney from the fireplace two floors down. Maggie looked away from the chimney and leaned forward and checked what she'd typed. The chimney wasn't red, really, it only appeared red in the bad light. In daylight, with no rain falling, it was more of an orange.

The huge oak desk sat on an oriental rug in the middle of the attic floor, flanked by more rugs, those rugs in turn flanked by sealed wooden boxes and gunnysacks and bales and a scattering of containers miscellaneous and nameless. And yet for all the colour in the rugs and the garish print in strange alphabets on the boxes and bales, the room was impossibly dark, foreboding —

Foreboding, nonsense. Maggie typed x's across the word. Stop inventing, she typed. George is a botanist. He ships specimens back from the rain forests he goes to Asia to study, and then instead of studying them, he goes back to Asia to find more.

An old brown leather-covered sofa, under the black dormer windows behind her, seemed determined to climb through one of the windows and jump.

This Inez, Maggie typed, is the pizza don of this humdrum, hooligan, soggy city. The pizza king is a lady, with a pistol under her pillow, and the rain falls all around. A beautiful lady she is, with a fleet of submarines to deliver pizza into the sleeping city's cheese and tomato and pepperoni dreams. And sometime near dawn she chains her criminal lover to her bed.

I hate her, she typed. Let it all hang out. I hate her and I want to meet her.

Two floors down, the doorbell rang at the exact time Tom Bludgett had promised it would ring. Bludgett and his invitation to dinner. Just when she was getting into a delicious, wonderful state of being totally pissed off, he had to come ringing the doorbell to say, *Obiter. Obiter dicta,* Maggie Wilder. Not to the point, Maggie Wilder.

She would not take off the dress before she went to answer the door.

But I should, she told herself; I should go change. I should not let Thomas Bludgett see the dress that he so wants to take possession of, power over, if only so he can helplessly tell Jack Deemer he has it. She hesitated. And yet I've been keeping it on just because I knew he was going to ring the bell. I want to hear what he'll say. What I'll say.

She pressed her fingers together, not letting the wooden rail slide cool and smooth under the curl of her left hand. She tramped down the stairway, wanting him to hear her footsteps. Bludgett, on the porch, dumb and waiting. Disturbing. Summoning. Playing out his role as the insomniac avoider of the world he claimed so loftily to understand. He didn't dare sleep, for fear of losing the control he liked to believe was his.

The dreamless man, there on her doorstep.

"Hello. Hope I'm not early."

Bludgett refused to acknowledge that he so much as noticed the dress. He did not once glance at the dress; he did not turn his head to speak while he made his way toward the kitchen. Maggie retaliated. She did not enter the kitchen at all; she turned from the doorway and went upstairs. And then, after she'd taken a shower, after she'd put on slacks and a sweater, letting him stew at the kitchen table, she called down the stairs to offer him a beer.

"I've helped myself," he called back.

It was that that made her say what she said. It was his careful or careless presumption that tipped her over the edge. She entered the kitchen before she spoke. Then she said, "I'm going to the mountains."

Bludgett looked puzzled.

She had only been toying with the idea. "Tomorrow," she said. "Or the day after. I'm going up to that Deadman Spring place where Papa B got into trouble."

"You are *what*?"

His surprise delighted her. "I'm going on a holiday up to that Kootenay Lake whatever — that spa." She paused, then added with relish, "No one has ever produced a body."

"Maggie —" Bludgett was trying at once to remain seated and to stand up. "I wouldn't advise it, Maggie."

"Thank you, Mr Lawyer. Even if you pretend you aren't a Mr Lawyer. Even if you claim you prefer to fill out income tax forms for a few months and do nothing the rest of the sleepless time. But surely you know the fascination of the site of the crime."

"You can't go there, Maggie. I wouldn't advise it. You mustn't."

"What's going to stop me?"

"I dread to think what might stop you." He tested his upper teeth with his tongue. "Or how."

"The long arm of the law? The powerful authorities to whose front doors the murderer on occasion delivers their evening meal?" Maggie opened the fridge and saw in front of the bottles of beer a head of lettuce, brown and slimy. "Perhaps we should eat here. We could send out for pizza."

"You can't go," Bludgett said. "You really shouldn't." He was offering her a bottle opener.

"It's a twist-off cap." She opened a bottle of Kokanee for herself but didn't take a drink.

"And are you going alone? Or are you taking the police with you?"

"Should I take them along for protection?"

"You be the judge."

"Funny, Thomas. You're a scream."

"You're being a fool, Maggie."

"Come along with me, if you dare." She regretted saying that, then added, "That wasn't a proposition."

"This is my busy season."

"I forgot. Or perhaps I couldn't tell."

"Besides," he said, "I never leave the city. It's one of my rules. I haven't been outside the city limits since the day I went on the inactive list as a lawyer."

"That fits. Your paralysis is geographical, along with being moral, physical, and emotional." She hated the way he liked to be attacked. "What kind of pizza this time?"

"We're going out," he said. "I might as well show you how to drive my car. That way you can take Josie and Ida with you."

Damn him, he was winning again. He was closing off her alternatives, shutting her down. You can use my car. Drive up into the mountains and get yourself killed in a February snowstorm, I could use the insurance money. I keep a car but I have nowhere to go. And he must know she'd been talking to Ida and Josie. The place was full of secrets, and yet no one, ever, made the slightest attempt at keeping a secret secret.

Maggie took a sip of beer.

She hadn't driven a car in days. It was one of the things she'd most liked doing during the past twenty-three years. The honeymoon drive east from Vancouver was one of the highs of her life, and going out for a drive on the dangerous twisting back roads of Upstate New York became her secret vice. Borrowing Bludgett's car, she could at least feel again the pull of a road, her body focused behind the wheel, her eyes skimming the world for the play of drifting images.

"I couldn't possibly take your car." She tried to defend her interest in doing what he suggested she do. "Henry wouldn't let me drive across the continent all by myself. It wasn't the danger that bothered him, believe me." She lifted a dry umbrella off the ironing board. "He got me to sell my car to help pay for this year of mine — this foolishness."

"Julie Magnuson," Bludgett said, not hurrying, "was driving a car that wasn't hers when she went over that cliff in Portugal."

"Thank you. Then I must borrow yours for sure."

"I thought that bit of information would persuade you for sure that you must go."

"But you said Julie had help with her accident. And you say you won't come along."

"Wear the wedding dress." He signalled that he would follow her toward the door. "At least take it with you. Just in case no one recognizes your interest in unnatural disasters."

And then the city was mauve, yellow, sometimes blue or green, in its hump of light. They drove. Maggie did the driving, trying to remember how to shift gears.

They were in the belly of a great whale, and the whale was the shape of light, barely sustaining itself against the Pacific darkness. Or the city was the whale and they were in the city, Maggie and Bludgett, and they drove in the wet, glowing night of the whale's sleeping. Somewhere the heart of the beautiful beast rested, and they drove in the long streets that glowed electric with the soft, erotic throb of sleep. The gentle rain, stalled in the heavy air, seemed visibly unable to fall.

"You've got the hang of it," Bludgett said. "Let's go somewhere?"

"Somewhere in the city, that is. Let's go to where we already are."

He ignored her little sarcasm. "You want to see Inez Catonio's house?"

His voice was too conciliatory. She was being humoured. He would distract her from her intention. Forget about your drive into the mountains, he was telling her.

"Where is this prison house of hers?"

"Up the hill from where you live. Just outside the gates of the university."

"So Ida and Josie have it right. That's where he goes, at dawn, after work."

"You've got it right."

"Papa B tells you all this?"

"He says nothing. Inez tells me."

Maggie, at that moment, liked the idea of Papa B being kept prisoner, voluntarily at dawn returning to Inez Catonio's house. What do they do together, how do they live, with him forever in hiding? Do they eat breakfast together, after the busy night? Does she undress him, slip him free of his strange, blue dress, let down his bun of hair, take him to bed with her? She wanted to ask and wouldn't.

"Let's not go there," Maggie said. "Not tonight. Let me show you one of my secret places."

She swung the car off the street that would take them to Inez's house and turned south. They got out of the car at the edge of the University Endowment Lands. They were on a city street, directly beside a forest.

"We're almost back to where you lived."

"Yes."

"You came here to play?"

She couldn't quite bring herself to answer him. They checked the signs again, under a street lamp, then stepped across the curb, Thomas tugging his fly tight shut as he did so. The light hardly followed them in under the cliff of the fir trees' shadows. It was simply dark in the forest. Maggie closed her eyes, then found in the forest the path that was in her memory.

"Hey." She called in the darkness to Bludgett. "We've hit it on our first try."

"There's nothing here."

"There's an opening in the forest. A riding stable. There's a riding stable in here somewhere. Come along."

They walked on, Maggie leading the way. "This is it," she said, the sound of exultation in her voice. She inhaled deeply. "You can smell the fir trees. The ferns. I swear I can smell horse manure. Horse sweat. Do you know how sweating horses smell?"

"There's nothing here, Maggie. This is like being in a cave. The riding stable, obviously, is long gone."

"That's not the point, Thomas. What does it matter if it's gone?"

"I would say it matters, Maggie."

He became an uneasy shadow, losing any hope of gesture. She could smell the warmth of him. It was a warmth she had not smelled in days, and she wanted it. Staying close at her side, he was at once persistent and lost. Maggie took his right hand. She touched the coldness of the back of his hand, the warmth inside the curled fingers. She put a hand inside his own to assure him. He was a tall, looming shadow that had lost its body but kept one hand.

She and her childhood friends, in their violent pubescence, stayed in that place in sleeping bags in a tent on a night that was at first too hot, then muggy, then cold and black. And nothing at all happened. The horses in the barn that was then a barn in that clearing in the forest stirred. That was all. Sometimes in the night a horse stomped a hoof on a wooden floor, or shifted its heavy body against the planks of a stall, or whinnied softly in reply to the whinnying of another horse.

Maggie, in that one night, had heard for the first time her father's aloneness. He handled horses, then, in the forests where he worked for the logging companies. Come home, he sat in silence, listening. A sleeping, standing horse could bruise itself in its own dull sleep. She heard the threat as a sound on the lids of her closed eyes. She could not in the morning tell if she had slept or lain awake through the whole night, but she had listened. She had listened with her father for the sounds of horses. She had wanted to tell him that she knew.

"This is the place," she said.

When Bludgett let go of her hand and tried to embrace her she shied away. Bludgett stumbled loosely against the directions. He said to the darkness around him that he wanted to make love. His voice in the darkness said it had not made love in a long time. It spoke an invitation. Wet grass, it said. Ferns. Pine boughs and fir.

"You're afraid," she said. "You're afraid I'll say yes."

"That's right," he said. "So say it."

"Stop dreaming, Thomas."

He was trying to approach her voice. "Keep talking," he said.

She refused to speak. She remembered her mother, never once entering this forest that was so near their house. She wouldn't move; she hardly breathed.

"This is childish," said Bludgett. He tried to sound dismissive, but his voice said he wanted to be reassured. "We're going to have one hard time finding our way out of here. . . . Where are you taking us?"

Maggie said nothing.

"This is stupidly dangerous," Bludgett said, "this forest gets cold at night, we could end up with hypothermia." And then when he tried to listen for her reply and heard nothing he laughed giddily to himself. "I think I heard —" He was silent, waiting again for

Maggie. She made no sound; she might have been gone. "Maggie? Listen. I heard a horse. I swear — there's a horse here on this trail. Maggie —"

And then the sound of the violence of his crashing down exploded against the dark. When he found his voice he was speaking from the forest floor. He was groaning and talking and groaning. He was trying to tell Maggie that a horse, moving down the path, had hit him. He had smelled the horse before it hit him. He had felt the hair of the horse's mane against his face; he was certain he had felt a hoof strike his own left foot.

He lay on the wet earth. Only after he had tried in vain for a long time to get Maggie to respond did he get to his feet and with his muddy hands grope his way toward the street and his car.

Maggie was sitting in the car, behind the steering wheel.

"Thanks a lot," Bludgett said. "Thanks a fucking lot."

Maggie said nothing. She started the car.

A light came on in the car when Bludgett opened the door on the passenger's side. He had a bloody nose. His face and his hands, along with the front of his sweater, were bloodied and smeared with wet soil and the green of leaves and needles and ferns.

"My shoulder." Bludgett stopped tugging at the seatbelt. "I can hardly move my arm. That damned fool horse." He was holding his left shoulder and telling Maggie again, in the dark, a moving horse had blindly struck him.

"You're making things up," Maggie said.

She drove him back to his apartment and guided him up the two flights of stairs and let him make tea for himself while she watched him learn to use his injured shoulder, and then, eagerly, she drove the borrowed car back to her house.

•

5

At first they were only leaving, not going anywhere, the three women. The departure was enough, and it was Josie who once in a while glanced through the rear window, reporting on the disappeared city and the disappearing suburbs, the leafless raspberry canes, cattle fading into the glaze of flooded fields, the bare hop trellises framing fog.

They drove in the shadowless light of the February morning. They lifted eastward up the long, wet valley of the Fraser, the highway under the Pontiac's wheels a loud and hissing whine. Inland they drove, watching the mountains ahead, where the clouds and the peaks met and dissolved against each other. They watched for Mount Baker and couldn't find it in the overcast and the gloom. The invisible sun hardly bothered Maggie's eyes. She drove, Ida beside her with a folded map on her lap and asking questions, Josie in the back seat with a basket of lunch, not watching the road at all and trying to count white-faced steers.

Somewhere past the town of Hope, getting into the mountains in a serious way, they saw where snow-slides marked their winter designs onto acres of rock-slide rubble. Maggie wasn't ready for the black ice. It was a cold day, and yet warm too. For an instant she lost control of the car and almost went off the road.

"Is this how Julie Magnuson had her accident?" Josie asked.

"There wasn't any snow in Portugal." Ida was becoming impatient with Josie's intrusions. "Portugal is on the equator," she added.

Maggie said nothing, grateful for the distraction. They were her guides, these two old women. "Portugal —" Maggie started to explain, then stopped. The Algarve. She thought of Julie Magnuson, a woman from the eastern slopes of the Rocky Mountains, driving one morning the mountainous roads of the Algarve, headed God knows where. . . . Going to meet a lover? Leaving a lover? Going somewhere to be alone with her terror at her own aloneness? Going to the site of the crime and finding the crime was her own death?

"Black ice," Josie said. "Maybe there was black ice, even if there wasn't snow. Is there black ice on Portuguese roads, Maggie?"

It was that way while they drove, up and over mountains and back into valleys. They were four hours out of Vancouver when they dropped down into a valley, the calendar tumbled out of winter and back to yellow grass and leafless orchards and sagebrush flats. They stopped at the edge of the highway and peed in a ditch in the dazzling sunlight. They opened their basket of lunch and drank coffee from the thermos Ida had filled the night before, courtesy of Midnight Pizza.

And then, after a lunch that put Josie to sleep in the back seat, they climbed again, up toward Anarchist Summit. Snow was falling, snow that was light and dry. They turned a corner and drove straight onto a trackless white road. A snowplough roared toward them. The shower of snow from the plough's blade was a plume of hard white sugar breaking from a saw.

Josie, startled out of her dozing in the back seat, spoke to the back of Maggie's head. "Did you bring the dress?"

Maggie had not been able, ever, to mention the dress.

"Mr Bludgett said you would," Josie said.

"I have the dress with me. It's in one of my bags in the trunk. I can't talk about it. But I'm going to show you. That's what I had planned to do."

She had planned to surprise Josie and Ida, and herself too, by putting on the dress and letting them see it. That way she wouldn't have to explain at all.

"You should have told us, Maggie," Josie said. "We're not mind readers."

Maggie steered too busily on the white road, making the car swerve. Perhaps she had brought Josie all this way simply to ask some questions of her own. And now they were in the mountains, driving too fast on a road that had lost its direction to the snow-filled trees, to the cliffs that leaned away from, toward, the road.

"Christ on a crutch." Ida was peering out her window, down the rock slope at the edge of the road. "The last damned thing we need in this car is that dress. It's double-digit bad luck."

Josie agreed vigorously. "Bad luck is bad luck."

"Send it back to Jack Deemer." Ida turned to Maggie. "Mail it to him. Along with a bomb."

"He's not going to get it."

"Somebody is. Going to get it."

Maggie wanted to say, it does wonders for me, I put it on and something happens. I haven't told you this. I meant to tell you. I was planning to tell you everything.

"That dress," Josie said. "The woman who got married in it got married to a monster."

"Maybe he was exactly what the bride wanted."

"Deemer!"

"I didn't say Deemer."

Josie leaned to Maggie's left ear. "Maggie, listen. Nobody liked Jack Deemer. He was about as popular as a fog. And he was a sly one. He never hunted. But he stole elk from the poachers. He stole booze from the bootleggers' shacks. And then went out and sold it."

Maggie laughed. "I take it he got caught."

"He'd steal the sweat from the crack of your ass," said Ida. "Just let that guy cross my path."

They were laughing together, the women, when abruptly Maggie swerved to avoid a semi that had jackknifed on the highway. The driver, setting out a flare, dived into the ditch to avoid being hit.

Just that suddenly the snow turned to rain.

"Shouldn't we stop?" Ida said.

Maggie shook her head. "We can't." She pointed into the rain. "Here's another truck now."

The car's headlights took them under the snow line again, the white at the sides of the road went black. The tires hissed in running water. Day and night, winter and spring tumbled against each other. Maggie drove numbly, her neck muscles pulling at her eyes. She couldn't talk, she couldn't bear to listen while Ida and Josie talked about Jack Deemer and his tricks, about Fish and how he didn't show up on the day of the wedding and how he gave up his career as a mining engineer and took to looking after Deadman Spring for Jack Deemer.

And then the roadside sign was there. The headlights, for an instant on a curve, caught its square absurdity, and Ida and Josie shouted.

"Nelson," Josie said. "We're here!"

They crossed a bridge; they turned into a cut through rock and made a left turn, all three of them watching for the names of streets, Maggie watching the traffic signals as well, in the rain and the dark. A city of ten thousand people, and every one of them gone to bed, apparently.

"Whoa," Ida said. She read the sign on a wall. "Bed and breakfast, fifteen dollars and up."

It was the hotel where they had their reservations. The Heritage Inn. Maggie swung hard to the right, into the small parking lot under the advertisement.

Josie and Ida burst into applause.

"My back teeth are floating." Ida undid her belt. "And on top of that I need a drink."

They checked in. Ida noticed the lounge, The Library; she suggested they leave their bags behind the desk and head straight for the bar.

"Not on your life." Josie touched a handkerchief to her nose. "I want Maggie to put on her dress. Let's do this in style."

"No way," Maggie said.

When she got to her room she unpacked the dress; she hung it on a hanger in order to brush it smooth. She touched her fingers across the weave of cloth behind pale blue gentians and elegant white crows. She touched at pale blue windows floating in a white sky.

Maggie hung up the dress and closed the closet door. She went quickly to the bathroom and then down to the lounge. The waitress took her to a table in front of the fireplace where Josie and Ida, their backs turned toward the flames, were trying to decide what to order.

The wicker furniture in the dark, ornate room was set on oriental rugs. On the walls were bookshelves crowded with discarded books. Two square pillars in the middle of the room had on them each four plaster figures of bare-breasted women holding up the ornate ceiling as if by painful effort.

Josie and Ida ordered hot rum with cinnamon sticks and took the two wicker chairs nearest the fire.

"Cutty Sark with lots of soda," Maggie said. She too sat down. "Wait. Hold the soda. One ice cube."

And that was when Fish announced his presence.

"Make mine a Kokanee," he said.

The man standing behind Josie's chair was aware only of Josie, it appeared at first. Josie was looking up at the fake beams of the ceiling that held between them billows of paisley. The man who bent over her chair and looked down into her face was waiting with suppressed anticipation to be recognized.

"Josie Pavich?" he asked.

Josie, her head still tilted back, waited.

"Remember me?"

Josie shook her head.

"Up there in the Coal Branch country. Back in Alberta. When I was a kid. Your dad took me down into the mines, taught me how to mine coal."

"Fish!" Josie leaned forward and pushed herself out of the chair. "Fish! We're on our way to visit you. We're coming to see you tomorrow. This is wonderful, Fish. My God you look old."

"I work at it."

Josie was making introductions, talking all the while: "This is Fish, Maggie. We grew up together. Except that I'm older than he is. By a long shot. You look good in grey hair, Fish. Maggie, this is Fish. This is Ida." She was still pointing at Fish. She laughed and Ida laughed.

Maggie's plan had gone awry. She had planned to surprise the man right there at Deadman Spring, arrive in the morning, confront him, ask questions, demand to know what had happened and why and where.

They were talking, Fish and Josie, about the Coal Branch, about how she didn't look a day older. Maggie turned and followed the waitress and stood at the bar while the bartender poured her a double scotch. Ida was joining in the conversation and Fish was nodding, to Ida, to Josie, to Ida. Maggie, sipping her drink, retreated to a bookshelf, the shelf supported by pale plaster heads set into the red floral design on the royal blue wallpaper. She wanted to duck down under the shelf and hide long enough to gather her wits about her.

She pulled a book off a shelf and opened it, then looked over the open book at Fish. He was blocky, muscular, a biggish man with a grey beard and tanned skin. He was wearing a wool toque, a denim jacket, jeans, work boots. For all his size and presence, he seemed to be trying to remain inconspicuous.

Josie was calling over to Maggie. "When are we getting there, Maggie?"

Damn, Maggie thought. She had unexpectedly emptied her glass. She pretended not to have heard and went toward the bar.

"The spa is practically deserted. We'll have it all to ourselves." Josie couldn't believe their good fortune. "Did you hear that, Maggie? He says we can soak for hours."

It was all supposed to be a secret. And instead Josie and Ida were organizing a reception.

"There's a woman there now," Fish said, calling toward the bar and Maggie. "A photographer. You'll have to meet her. She's been looking for the corpse, off and on, for the past four years."

Maggie returned to the table and sat down. They were within a few kilometres of the spa. It would be foolish to turn back. Among other things, she couldn't possibly face Bludgett. He'd rejoice, after he'd finished being sarcastic.

Fish sat down at the table in the chair farthest from Maggie's. "This woman with all the cameras is making a film of the lake bottom. Every damned inch of the lake bottom where the corpse might have got silted over or snagged. Some kind of a nut."

Maggie glanced up from the fire to the tall photograph above the fireplace, a nude woman standing in profile, holding with both hands a long ribbon, the ribbon looped in a collapsed circle around the back of her head. A woman dressing, she decided, not undressing but dressing. Getting ready to put on a wedding dress.

Maggie spoke across the low table and their drinks to Fish. "Do you have a boat?"

"You won't need a boat to sit in the pool."

"Josie and Ida can sit in the pool. I want to see where Dr De Medeiros drowned."

"I wouldn't recommend it."

"You do have a boat, I can tell."

"If you can call it that. It's a little car-topper, with a kicker at one end. Good for summer fun. I wouldn't so much as get it wet at this time of year."

"I'll hire you. Tomorrow morning."

"This isn't summer."

Josie, pointing conspicuously at Ida's hands, leaned into the conversation. "Ida and I are staying in the pool. Aren't we, Ida?"

"Speak for yourself, Josie."

Fish was shaking his head. "You'd have to cross the lake. It's almost straight across the lake from Deadman, that spot. First off, my boat isn't covered. Second, the cabin over there is closed for the season."

That was when Ida had her turn. "Maggie," she said, "you'd be beautiful. In an open boat. Crossing the lake in a mist. Wearing your wedding dress. Going to meet your lover."

"Not a lake," Josie said. "A mountain stream. Like on the dress."

Fish didn't blink an eye. He pulled the wool toque down to and then over his thick eyebrows and puckered his mouth.

"You look," Josie said, "like someone just asked you to kiss a trout."

And then Josie was explaining. To Maggie. To Ida. She explained that Fish had asked for one small detail to be included in the flow and drift of details on the dress. While Julie Magnuson went on delaying her decision, while she, Josie Pavich, went on preparing the dress and preparing it again, he asked for one explicit detail. Josie embroidered all the soft colours of the dress into the scales of a rainbow trout, the trout in a mountain stream, the stream and its flowered banks under a hint of mountains, the wide range of mountains under a raft of cumulus clouds, windows afloat among the clouds.

Josie stopped talking and sipped her hot rum. "That was all for you," she said. To Fish.

He glanced from Josie to Ida to Maggie. His tongue had become too big for his mouth. Or too small.

It's an albatross, Maggie thought. That wedding dress. It's a curse, an abomination.

Fish bowed awkwardly toward Maggie. "This is why you're here then," he said. He explained no further; he asked for no explanation. He put down his beer bottle and pulled his toque down over his ears.

The three women did not turn to watch Fish go through the door and disappear.

"You shouldn't have done that to him," Maggie said. She was looking around now, to catch the waitress's attention.

"I was doing my best," Josie said. "That's all I intended."

"He deserved it," Ida said. "He had his chance."

The morning dark was slow to dissolve. Maggie showed up late for breakfast in the General Store Restaurant, across the foyer from The Library. She had a black, blistering, murderous headache.

The walls and pillars of the restaurant were hung with ladles and ice tongs and cowbells, with old tin pails labelled Burns' Carnation Brand Shortening and Swift's Jewel Brand Shortening. Josie craning her neck around while Ida pointed and reminisced.

"Instruments of torture," Maggie said.

Ida went on pointing. "You see that big granite coffee pot hanging up there from the ceiling? Inez Catonio's mother and I kept two of those full, in the cookhouse we ran where she met her husband. He was a rancher doing winter work in a logging camp while he figured out how to get rich."

Maggie groaned. Looking up made her dizzy. She couldn't lift her gaze higher than the ketchup bottles set on the counter beneath a gopher trap nailed to the square pillar. She counted. Six bottles of Heinz. She counted the high stools ranged empty and in a row along the counter. Seven. The world was measurable, countable, accountable; all the men in her life, and that included Henry Ketch and Tom Bludgett and Papa B and Fish, be damned for driving her to drink.

She ordered something called Song's Pancakes from the menu and then Josie and Ida decided they too wanted pancakes with maple syrup. Maggie let the waitress refill her coffee cup three times. They were losing time before they'd begun.

They were keeping their rooms for another night. They straggled empty-handed, the three women, out into the damp light of morning. On Elephant Mountain, to the west across West Arm, the snow line was down below Pulpit Rock.

Josie pointed up at the outcrop of rock on the mountainside. "The waitress said that's their weather forecaster around here. The snow line is low and the forecast bad."

Ida slipped and fell in the parking lot. "Damned black ice."

Maggie was helping her to her feet. "You don't want to go? If we're going to turn back, now is the time."

Ida said nothing.

"Well?"

Maggie turned to Josie. "What do you think?"

"I think we're going to get ourselves killed. But we have to go. Ida thinks Fish is cute."

"And you don't."

"He used to be a knockout. Now he looks like a dishrag."

"I'll cast the deciding vote," Maggie said. "I think that spa water is going to be a treat."

"You're cheating, Maggie," said Ida. "What do you really think?"

"I think Fish has something up his sleeve. You can see it in his face."

They drove through town. They crossed over a bright green bridge, and there on dry land above the road was a wheelhouse, along with two decks of an old steamboat, turned into a three-story house.

"The world is upside down here," Josie said. "I'm warning you."

They used the shoreline as a map. Approaching a ferry landing, they swerved away, turned north onto a branch road, and followed along the western shore of the lake. Someone had fastened neckties to the miles of telephone poles along the winding road. Just once, in a break in the clouds, Maggie, busy driving, caught a glimpse of Mount Loki, dazzling and high, looming white over the black lake and the steep shoreline and the comic row of necktie-wearing telephone poles.

She almost missed the sign. Small and crudely printed, it hung from the arm of a post on the left shoulder of the road, under the wall of an empty wooden building on which was printed in more elegant but faded letters, G. B. FLETCHER GENERAL MERCHANT. The sign she almost missed read, Deadman Spring.

The forest and the old buildings on the steep hillside to her left were disintegrating into shreds of mist. The small buildings on her right seemed to have just then stepped back off the road; absurd in the bright colours of their false fronts, they teetered over the black lake behind and below them.

Fish was standing directly in the middle of the road.

Maggie pretended at first to be about to hit him, then swerved and stopped. She turned down her window.

Fish spoke first. "This isn't a good idea."

"That's why you're out here waiting for us."

"I came here to tell you to turn back while you still have time." He turned away.

"Fish wants us here," Josie said. "Otherwise he'd be in Alaska by now. That's how he is."

"He's cuter than I thought he was," Ida said. "And twice as stubborn as he is cute."

"He isn't stubborn enough for his own good," Josie said.

"He's stubborn as an ox."

On foot, taking his own good time, Fish led them. The gravel trail wound off the highway, down toward the lakeshore. Maggie eased the car down the trail, the dried reeds higher than the car's windows. The car broke into a small clearing, in front of Fish's old trailer. The lake was dark and calm, the sky overcast, the peaks of the mountains across the lake lost from sight in the overcast sky.

The trailer was up on cement blocks. Fish let the three women in through the narrow aluminum doorway. The trailer inside was so sparsely furnished, so meticulously neat, it seemed there might be no one living in it at all. Fish showed Josie and Ida the food in the small fridge, the cooler that would need filling with sandwiches and fruit.

"I take it we're going somewhere," Ida said.

"Your idea. Not mine." Fish took down four mugs from a cabinet and went to the door, if only to make room in the trailer.

Maggie followed him outside. The pain behind her eyes was easing, after the drive. A mug of coffee in one hand, she scrambled up and found a place to sit on a high hump of rock near the shore.

The lake from north to south seemed infinite, either end disappearing into dark mist. Across the lake she saw at first only green forest under the row of white peaks, a barely sketched-in line of rock and beach between the forest and the black water.

Then her eyes caught the detail that she wasn't somehow expecting. The grouped pilings were there, three miles across the lake, somewhat to the south of where she had been looking. She had expected tall, thick pilings that loomed grey and stark against the dark of the forest above the beach. Instead, seen from a distance, they were delicate, magical, an intricate pattern of toothpicks on the edge of the dark lake.

Fish eased the boat into the water. It looked to Maggie like a badly designed bathtub. Fish said nothing, puttering around along the shoreline. He went into the trailer, when Ida called him, to have fresh coffee.

Maggie waited without impatience. Only when she went to the trailer for another cup of coffee did Fish and Josie and Ida come out, taking Maggie's appearance as a sign that she was in a hurry.

The four of them together began to load the food and gasoline and extra clothing into the boat. Trust three women from the coast, Fish said, to organize an expedition and forget to bring parkas. He showed them how to put on the red and yellow life jackets by putting on his own. Ida was to sit across from him in the stern of the small aluminum boat, the tiller of the outboard motor between them. She crawled stiffly past the red gas tank and sat down. Josie was next into the boat. She sat amidships, reaching to hold the shipped oars on either side of her unsteady seat. Fish crawled past her and sat down across from Ida and asked Maggie to give the boat a push and at the same time to hop in and sit in the bow.

The motor started easily. They backed away from shore, turning. They began to move out toward open water.

"Keep your bodies low," Fish said. "Sit low. We've got too much of a load. This is stupid."

"We know that," Josie said. "That's why we're bringing you along."

Fish talked over the whine of the small Mercury, naming for Ida and Josie the peaks, the bays, the beaches. He was, for all his complaining, exhilarated. He began to talk about spas, how they helped people, how they would help Ida and Josie — once we get back from this foolish boat ride, he added. He told them of other spas, the old spas in Europe, the spas of Italy, of Ancient Rome. Josie told him he sounded like the famous spa doctor who had drowned here in this lake. If spas are so good for you, she wanted to know, how come he was dead?

Maggie couldn't bring herself to look away from the distant pilings. They were taller now, in the water, grey-black, each composed of huge thick logs bound together, all grouped to make a landing place and a loading place for steamboats that had long since disappeared. Maggie could make out now the piling that had on its flat top the nest of an osprey. She wanted to stand up, the better to see, but didn't dare, sensing the sharp, compelling eyes of Fish at her back.

It was little more than a half-hour after their departure when Fish slowed the motor. "Right along here somewhere," he said, in the abrupt quiet, "we can see the hulk of the *Kokanee*. The old sternwheeler. She went down here, would you believe" — he indicated the calm of the water, the stillness of the air — "capsized by wet snow. Maybe thirty years ago. Went down like a rock."

They peered over the sides of the car-topper, all of them, looking for the wreck. Fish was explaining, "Watch for the paddle wheel. That or the wheelhouse. She's on her side. Some people think the body got caught in the wreck. That's why it didn't come up. That's why Karen is here, with her newfangled camera. Lower it into the water. It doesn't stir up the muck."

He hadn't named the photographer before. Maggie was struck by the ease with which he talked about her. The familiarity. Karen was, apparently, no stranger to Fish. Or they were at once strangers and friends. Maggie thought of Bludgett, with his books and his sleepless nights and his uneasy demands that he didn't want satisfied. She thought of Henry, looking for icons, refusing to look beyond the bounds of Mount Athos to where other icons might be.

And just then Josie spotted the dim outline of the boat. She tried to indicate to the others what she saw, but no one else could see it. Fish, to indicate to Josie that he believed her, swung the small boat in a circle around the spot she pointed toward in the dark water.

Fish swung the boat in one circle, and then in another. "This is how Manny came in for his landing. But he was watching the shore, not the wreck." Fish was steering with his right hand, pointing with his left. "Julie's dwarf doctor. He was standing up and steering his outboard and trying to spot the cabin. Billy was up there in that cabin."

Maggie hadn't until then noticed the cabin, almost concealed by trees on a cliff to the south of the small open beach.

"Billy was up there with his rifle." Fish corrected himself. "He didn't own a rifle. There was a rifle in the cabin." Fish, his head tilted back, groaned as he spoke. "He claimed in some journals he left that he fired a shot just to steer the doctor away from a couple of young ospreys in that nest up there."

"Whoa."

Not watching, watching only the water and the cabin, Fish had almost hit a piling. The pilings loomed enormous straight up over the boat.

Fish pointed up at the far tops of the pilings. The women tilted back their heads to look up at the top of the nearest piling. Sticks and grass indicated the presence of a nest. Above the nest the thick clouds closed the sky.

"You see," Fish said again, pointing back now at the water they'd just crossed, "De Medeiros was standing up in his canoe. He had to stand up, he was a tiny little guy. He had his outboard running slow, he was heading toward that piling." Fish was explaining, pointing, gesturing. He indicated the bow of his own boat, where Maggie sat hunched, delicately balancing herself against the boat's uncertainty.

"You see the bow? Imagine a kind of crest painted there. A bull's-eye. The canoe belonged to a man who had only one eye. That's why he painted one on one side of his canoe, but not on the other."

Maggie tried to glance over the side of the boat's bow, as if this might be the boat that De Medeiros had crossed the lake in.

"Bam!" Fish said.

The violence of the boat's collision with the sand almost pitched Maggie over the bow.

They were scrambling, then, as the motor went dead, out of the boat, out of their life jackets. Fish gave them each something to carry, a plastic water bottle, rain gear, a bag of fruit. He picked up the cooler.

They crossed the open beach and walked in single file through the high undergrowth, Fish leading the way. He stopped and waited, then bent again to the steep climb up toward the cliff's edge, carrying the cooler and some extra jackets. He put down his load and knocked at his pockets for a key to the door, but by then the women had found the simple plank deck at the front of the cabin and were looking down onto the beach where they'd landed.

They were looking down onto the curve of the beach and its cluster of pilings. The arranged pilings found their entire focus in the osprey nest. That one nest invited protection, with ships and cannons if necessary. With violence and secrecy and subterfuge. They saw that, the three women. They understood Papa B and were on his side. He had wanted to send away the approaching canoe, the two young ospreys poised there on that high piling, ready to risk their first flight, their leap into the air or their fall into the water.

Fish came out of the cabin with chairs. He unfolded canvas deck chairs for Ida and Josie. Maggie sat down on a wooden bench at the wooden table. Fish accepted the third chair, then, as his own.

"It was there at that table," Fish said to Maggie, "that Billy wrote the journal entries that put his neck in the noose. He described how he fired the rifle and how Dr De Medeiros fell out of the canoe and into the water — and didn't come up once, let alone three times. Billy wrote the journal entry and put a rock on the pages. And then he too disappeared."

Maggie touched the surface of the table, liking the roughness of the weathered wood under her fingertips. She liked wood. She tried not to think of Papa B, at the table, putting his neck in the noose. Billy, as Fish called him. He had other names as well as other lives, her Papa B. But he liked to sit at a table and feel the grain of the wood under his fingertips.

"Did they take flight?" Josie said.

Fish looked puzzled. "Who?"

"The young ospreys. Did they manage to fly?"

"The shot that Billy fired. It sent them into the air. They never looked back."

"Hurray!" they said together, Josie and Ida.

Maggie glanced down again at the osprey nest, then across the lake to Deadman Spring, small under its backdrop of forest and white mountain peaks.

"De Medeiros," Fish said, "didn't show up at Deadman Spring that night. He'd come over here to see Billy, who was in seclusion of some sort. Living in this cabin." He paused. "Something to do with . . . a broken heart."

Maggie and the two women in their deck chairs exchanged smiles.

"I mean it," Fish said. "There is such an ailment. It makes people walk around dead."

"You were suspicious," Ida said, "just because De Medeiros was away for one night?"

"We were worried. Concerned. Manny wasn't your do-it-yourself kind of man. We thought maybe he'd stayed the night with Billy. But then he didn't come back next morning either. So that afternoon three of us came over, Karen Strike and me and the one-eyed fellow who owned this cabin at the time." Now it was Fish who smiled a knowing smile, his glance meeting Josie's. "Deemer was very decent about it. He told the owner he could either sell the cabin or watch it burn down."

"It's still here," Ida said.

"That one-eyed fellow stayed on the beach." Fish pointed. "Karen and I climbed up the path. . . . Actually, she stopped at the biffy on the way." He pointed at a wall of firs. "There's an outhouse in there, if you're looking for one. I came up to the cabin. There was nobody here. Not hide nor hair of De Medeiros. Not a trace of Billy either."

"There was a trace," Josie said. "You said the journal was there on the table."

Fish agreed. "I didn't notice it right then. I thought maybe they were out for a walk, Billy and De Medeiros. Then this one-eyed guy comes hollering up from the beach because, he shouts, there's a bullet hole in the bow of his brand-new canoe."

"And after the doctor went overboard and didn't come up," Maggie said, "this Billy fellow sat down right here and wrote in a journal what had just happened and left the journal right here on this table?"

"He left it right there where your elbows are. Under a rock. The journal was there. He was gone."

"I'd say he's trying to get caught," Maggie said. "Trying to get his neck into a noose."

Fish shook his head. "Then why can't anybody find him?"

6

They were silent, the three women, there on the cabin's deck. Maybe they were listening for a gun to go off. But the only sound was the ravens, and, believe me, when you're out in the bush, that's racket enough. Sometimes it sounds like a mixture, half curiosity, half disgust. That's how it sounds to me. And, yes, I am the Jack Deemer people mention with curiosity and disgust. You don't put together a collection of collections without first putting together a little heap of the stuff that buys collections. Once in a while I had to make the rules fit the occasion.

But I was always good to Billy Dorfendorf. He was a kid from the bald prairies who got himself an education in the ways of museums and then got a job with me as an agent, finding collections for my collection of collections. And I never once checked on his expense accounts, I left that to one of my accountants and then didn't read the reports. He had a nose for the perfect collections, that Billy, maybe because he didn't know anything about history. What he looked at was what he saw. That's how he always struck me.

Dorf. That's what I called him. He was absolutely the best agent I ever employed. He once came back from Mongolia, more dead than alive, with a collection of lariats that would have been the envy of Genghis Khan. He found a collection of doorways in Spain that would have filled the holds of all of Columbus's ships. Sir William Burrell, that Scottish collector of considerable means, would have traded me a ton of French lace for the collection of fragments of woven cloth my Dorf brought back from Peru. And then he phoned one day from an English village, and he said he was on his way to a spa in a Portuguese town.

My wife was in that town at the time — Luso. She was there at her favourite spa with her favourite doctor.

For whatever reason, I have never to this day been to the place across from Deadman Spring where Billy Dorfendorf fired the rifle that wasn't his. I sent Karen there, with a carload lot of cameras new and old. I sent her to photograph the canoe, and then I sent her back again, to film the beach, the landing place, the single piling on which the ospreys hatched their own mysterious plots as well as their eggs. I sent her in summer. I sent her back in the spring and fall. I sent her back in winter too, when the water level is down, to photograph the pilings all over again, the nest, the lakeshore seen from the lake, the lake seen from the cabin above. And while my sight faltered, as it sometimes does, I went on studying the clues she brought back in cans and packages to my warehouse shelves. Sooner or later. That was our motto, and a useful one too. Sooner or later.

I was, at the time of Maggie's impetuous visit, employing Karen to photograph a square mile of lake bed, a tedious task surely, and yet a task that in its own unlikely way bore fruit. Karen Strike and I — she was intent on making films and needed time and equipment. She needed money. I have money. I needed to stop the flow of time so I could take a close look. I wanted to know, I had to find out, why the coffin that Dr De Medeiros shipped back from Portugal came to my warehouses empty.

The sun fooled them. Somewhere in the middle of the afternoon the sun broke through the clouds and warmed the cabin deck into an illusion of summer. Josie and Ida, in their chairs, being waited on, eating too much, putting rum in their coffee, eating again, fell asleep. Maggie insisted on going for a walk, and Fish insisted on going with her. They poked along the beach, Maggie somehow persuaded she would find a corpse washed up on shore, for all the calmness of the water. Instead, she exhausted herself, and she too, back at the cabin, went in and lay down on a bunk and dozed off. It was Fish, knocking discreetly at the cabin door, who suggested that maybe they should get cracking. It was that word rather than any sound that startled Maggie awake.

Then she too heard the unnatural stillness that gave hint of approaching rain. She went out onto the deck and awakened Ida and Josie. She finished with one gulp her cup of cold coffee and rum. Ida and Josie asked for the path to the outhouse.

Fish and Maggie gathered together what belongings they'd carried up the cliffside path; Fish again led the way, this time down, into the forest, then out onto beach. It was Fish who held life jackets for each of the three women, Fish who helped them into waterproof coats, this in spite of the lake's calm.

The lake was eerily smooth, its surface a mirror that gave back everything, allowing no penetration at all.

"It looks like black ice," Ida said.

They were slow getting started. Maggie wanted to move among the pilings, studying the shadows under them, the stillness of the water. Fish let the motor idle, the boat hardly moving, while Maggie touched the rough wood of a piling, turned away, waited while the boat moved, touched another. When, finally, they headed out into open water, Fish sat in the stern leaning forward as if the wind had already hit them.

They were something like halfway across when the first rain, a moving wall, showed in the north end of the mountain trench that is the valley of the lake. It seemed far away; it seemed it might miss them entirely. Then, abruptly, the approaching shore blurred out of sight. It dissolved into a greyness that drew behind it the threat of a night that would fall before its time.

Maggie, her back to the Deadman shore, didn't notice. Crossing over the sunken boat had triggered her mind and she was imagining, if not the corpse, the beautiful white bones of Dr Manuel De Medeiros, tangled in the black water and a steamboat's broken decks. She wanted his ghost to rise like a column of spray. She wanted to row toward a dead lover, riding a small boat, wearing her wedding dress.

"We're risking our lives," Ida said, addressing her remark to no one in particular. "One time not far from Kitimat I went out to dump some potato peelings where the bears wouldn't come to eat them and I saw two men drown. Just like that. They were in a boat, fishing. A squall hit them. There wasn't a thing we could do."

The smooth lake was frothing white at the front edge of the storm's greyness. Maggie, seeing Josie signal, looked briefly over her left shoulder, then turned again toward the three figures huddled in the boat. She looked out over their bowed heads to the pilings beyond, where a last stroke of light opened the beach.

The gusting rain that hit her back was icy cold. Small waves leapt up round the boat.

"Shouldn't we run with it?" Ida said to Fish, over the sounds of the motor and the wind and the rain.

He shook his head. "We've half a mile to go. If we stay out here too long we're going to ice up."

Their heads were close together, yet they were shouting at each other, Ida and Fish. Maggie could hear Fish explaining, the spray would turn to ice. The rain was a freezing rain, the drops of water turning to ice on the aluminum of the boat, on the shipped wooden oars. Maggie noticed the ice on the hood of Josie's parka and touched a bare hand to the back of her own bared head and found beads of ice in her hair. Spray broke off the crests of the waves.

Fish slowed the motor. The blown crests of waves came over the starboard side of the boat. Ida moved her feet, then carefully moved them again, trying to stay out of the sloshing water.

Maggie thought of Bludgett and was grateful for his absence. He could injure himself by closing his eyes. She let herself guess how he would stand up in the stern, asserting his squinted eyes against the rain, teetering, losing his balance and catching it again and losing it —

They saw the boat, all three of them at once, Ida and Josie and Fish. They had been watching for any sign of the approaching shore and then they saw the boat that bore down on them out of the darkness of the storm. Ida and Josie, together, shouted to Fish, who at the same time saw what was happening and tried, helplessly, to shout at the approaching boat.

Maggie almost went overboard, turning to look. The ghostly white boat was coming straight at them. She raised an arm to signal. The invisible steersman in the high, rocketing boat seemed to take the raised arm as a beacon and aimed straight at it. Maggie, recoiling, tried to hide her arm.

Then the approaching boat was only too real. Its bow high out of the water, no faces showing in the windows of the cabin, it broke across the whitecaps. Fish swung his tiller, turning away from the oncoming boat and almost capsizing. The larger boat swung to make a correction too, lifting into a new trajectory, bearing down directly on the small car-topper and its four occupants.

The running lights on the approaching boat went off. The wave of water in its wake swept over the smaller boat.

"Hang on," Fish shouted. "Sit lower."

The outboard motor coughed and drowned. The small aluminum boat, losing its momentum, began to roll. Fish reached for an oar and lifted it and used it to swing the bow downwind. Ida and Maggie found pails and began to bail. Josie wrestled with the second oar.

Fish pulled the cord on the outboard motor. It started and stopped. He pulled again at the starting cord and the motor sputtered, caught. "Rocks," he shouted. He pointed. They could see a ladder that went straight up a cliff, into the storm itself.

And then the boat was beside them. The boat that had attempted to run them down was pulled close enough to offer protection to the four people in the car-topper; a woman came out of the cabin of the larger boat. With a careful, far swing of her right arm over her head she threw a coil of line. Fish shouted at Maggie to catch it. The line fell across Maggie's shoulders. Fish shouted again, to Maggie, telling her to knot the line into the metal ring on the car-topper's bow.

I didn't pay Karen Strike to play games with people's lives. Her maliciousness was her own, not mine, and, say what you will, her taunting of people with death by drowning was not my idea. Granted, the people in the boat had no legal justification for their reckless adventuring, and that included my employee Fish, who should have been on guard instead of in cahoots. He was ever my enemy, for all the care he took of Deadman Spring. Karen, on the other hand, had a little moral streak in her. Teach people to stay away from water by having them drown.

Maggie and Josie and Ida, naked in the spa pool, were become floating heads on the water's steaming surface. The warm mineral water was lit from beneath the surface, the air was dark. The steam turned into a roiling mist. The flakes of wet snow fell into the mist but never quite touched the water.

"Here," Maggie said. She'd found a cement bench, under the surface, where the water splashed hot into the pool from the cave beyond.

They were in the pool at Deadman Spring. But they might have been in the car-topper still, Ida and Josie, their boat sunk beneath them. They were seated side by side, watching Maggie who, in deeper water, clung to a ladder. The wind hissed in the invisible trees above the twin mouths of the cave.

Fish had taken away the women's clothes, to put them in dryers in the dark shadow that was the spa's main building.

A group of elderly men and women came out of the nearer entrance to the cave. The small light bulb just inside the cave's entrance lit briefly their naked bodies. They entered the pool like birds come to rest for the night and fell into a hushed talking. They were local

Doukhobors, speaking softly to each other in Russian. Maggie liked the consolation of the sound of their talk, the ease of her own not understanding.

She wanted to let herself cry. The two old women couldn't see her concern. They were indomitable. They were pleased with the way they'd silenced Fish, slipping out of all their cold, wet clothing. He'd picked up the soggy clothes and fled.

But now he was back. Maggie saw him, shadowy at the edge of the pool; he untied his boots and kicked them off. He took off his wet socks and wrung them out and dropped the twisted socks beside his boots. He turned his back and stripped down and backed into the pool wearing only his toque.

"Nice buns," Ida said.

Fish was talking before the tip of his beard got wet. "The whole crowd of them. Deemer and the little doctor and Billy B — Sometimes we called him Billy B. They were all in love with Julie Magnuson." He touched his mouth down into the water. "They'd go into that cave." He raised a hand out of the water and pointed toward the nearer entrance. "She was gone already by then, you understand. Deemer ordered the coffin shipped back from Portugal. He attended the funeral all by himself. But, after the funeral was over, he needed to have Billy and Manny with him, there in that cave."

"And you," Josie said.

Fish made no protest. "I was here too. We were all here." Then he went on, "They'd pretend they were healers, the three of them. But mostly they were trying to bring Julie Magnuson back to the world. You know what I mean? They believed themselves, each one of them, secretly, to be the only man she'd ever really loved."

When the camera flash for an instant offered its blink of light in the falling snow, Maggie realized that Karen was somewhere in the surrounding darkness.

Fish disappeared under the water. He seemed gone too long. A flurry of snow filled the air. Snow fell heavily, into the stilled space under the cliffside. The wind howled, up above the thickly falling snow. The flakes, touching the warm water, disappeared.

Maggie, watching the spot where Fish had let himself sink, was on the lake again. The boat was coming at them and over and over she raised an arm. A protest. An invitation. The apparition would run them down. Or swamp them. But they were wearing life jackets. The corpses would float crazily on the black water. Forever. They would float forever, and always just out of reach, four corpses. They would drift with the lake's currents, moved by the wind, unable to sink into the silence that was Manny's. She would be wearing her wedding dress.

The toque came to the surface. Fish's toque. And then his head was there too, his face and beard and mouth, and he was talking, as if he had dived far and deep for a new supply of words. Each effort at speech exhausted him. He gasped air into his lungs and then he was speaking.

"She's as crazy as old Deemer himself. He wants to collect everything in the world. She just wants an exact copy. When the world ends" — he gasped again for air — "she'll make a copy of that too. She'll make an exact copy of the end of the world. For Deemer to add to his collection of ends of the world." And then he said bitterly, "The way she's adding us."

Karen Strike asked no permission, said nothing. She was invisible and soundless, until her camera snatched out of the darkness its small, lightning record. After a flash the darkness was all the more intense, brightly black.

Fish buried his nakedness in the water. Maggie found herself siding with Karen, wanting to catch him off guard. She wanted to surprise him into sight, scare him into the misted, snow-filled air; she moved closer. She saw his nakedness, under the small, swaying waves; in the light from underwater bulbs she saw his penis, trapped and drowning, lifting itself up toward the air.

"I want to confront her. For threatening our lives."

"I talked to her," Fish said.

"And?"

"She says she saw us. She knew we were in trouble. She was coming to our rescue."

Maggie lifted her shoulders and breasts out of the water. "Pure bull."

Fish raised a hand from under the water's surface and wiped at his eyes. "She asked why you're here. 'Why is that woman *really* here?' she asked me."

"And what did you tell her?"

"I told her you have the wedding dress that Jack Deemer took back to Josie Pavich after he married Julie Magnuson."

"Good God," Maggie said. "She'll tell Jack Deemer. Don't you know that?"

"I know that." Fish had become aware that Maggie was looking down into the water, watching his floating body. He turned away. He turned his back to her.

Maggie put her hands on Fish's shoulders. She gave a thrust with her legs and at the same time using her arms pulled herself upward; she made it; she was sitting on his shoulders; she closed her thighs against his neck; she steadied herself; she let go of his hair, raised her arms.

Just as Fish sank out of sight, Karen snapped her picture.

Need I tell you that that was the first picture, ever, I saw of Maggie Wilder, her breasts delicately small, her face in a kind of ecstatic release. Is it possible to love a photograph?

Fish was not in the photograph at all. He had disappeared from sight. He was a man who waited. Perhaps waiting above all else is what renders us, each, invisible.

He did not so much as realize the photograph had been taken. After he dumped Maggie back into the pool and recovered his breath, he was nothing but business. He was a master at pretending that nothing had happened.

"When your clothes are dry," he said, to Josie and Ida, then to Maggie, "I'll drive you up to the Mermaid Lodge. I've made reservations for the three of you. You should stay there until morning. Get some decent rest. Then in the morning you can leave."

Ida and Josie were sunk to their mouths in the water, curing their ills. They listened in silence to each other's pleasure, breaking that silence only now and then, once to ask Fish for a bit more time. Falling snow touched at their hair and melted, and more snow fell, and melted. He said he would let them stay as long as they liked, but too much time in the hot water, he said, would make them sleep for hours.

7

And, next day, they slept through most of the long drive, Josie and Ida.

Vancouver was soggy, under a dark blanket of cloud that squashed the night onto the pavement. Maggie helped Josie and Ida carry their bags into Josie's small house. She caught a glimpse of the dress forms, headless and legless, there in the living room, where Josie sewed wedding dresses while Ida held a tape measure or found pins or looked for a missing spool of thread.

No, Maggie told them, she didn't have time for tea or a rye and ginger. The drive had been brutally long. It was too late at night for talk. It was too late at night for anything, she couldn't return Bludgett's car, not to-night.

Maggie was dazed with weariness. She stood in front of her own front door, unable to find the right key on the rings of keys that opened other doors and locks, in the house she could hardly remember having occupied with Henry and her two sons. Where was she? There was no light coming through the thick squares of glass in the door. She was almost certain she'd left on the hallway light. Then she found the key and turned the lock. She groped for the confusing row of buttons in their brass panel; the hallway light came on.

Maggie made a cup of coffee and then decided to drink it in the bathroom upstairs while she prepared to collapse into bed. The door to the attic, she noticed, climbing the stairs, was open. She was certain she never left that door open.

Or maybe, in her haste to be away, she had accidentally left it ajar. There was a light on in the attic, her desk lamp no doubt; she recognized the small haze of light over the dark of the stairwell.

Maggie went into her bedroom. She had to learn to live alone, get hold of her imagination. Josie and Ida would have laughed at her indecision, after all the determination of the long drive. She was weary beyond sleep. She was tempted to unpack the wedding dress and put it on and march up the attic steps and sit down at her typewriter.

Just wait a minute, she told herself. You are finding excuses. So find excuses. You couldn't possibly write a single note, the shape you are in. All you have to do —

Yes, she would do it. She would make notes while everything was right there, on the top of her memory. Maggie took off her sweater and slacks. She unpacked the wedding dress and put it on. She put on a pair of slippers. She gripped the coffee cup in her right hand and went out the bedroom door to the door that opened onto the attic steps. She marched loudly up the steps.

I, Jack Deemer, would have given a million dollars to be in Maggie's place that late night, a gun in my hand instead of a cup of coffee. And I bear no grudges, believe me, let the past be the past. All I want is to play out the show to its consequence, with justice and truth triumphant. My notion of a happy ending might have something to do with a hot gun barrel, but happiness takes many forms, doesn't it? Sooner or later.

The pizza man was there, seated at Maggie's desk. He glanced up as if surprised and perhaps just a little bit offended that she should elect, like a ghost, to appear in that attic.

Maggie's head was at floor level when she saw him. She stepped back and down a step, into the narrow, dark stairwell, disappearing. Then she told herself she must not retreat.

It seemed to her at first that he was busy cutting out paper dolls.

There he sat, his tall and flat-topped hat on the desk beside him. He glanced up from his sheet of paper and scissors, at her reappearance, at her second surfacing, as if her expected and unexpected arrival was at once an irritation and a relief. He was in danger of accidentally trimming his own beard.

Maggie was totally exhausted. Her feet were too heavy for all her remaining strength to raise. Her back and arms ached with the pull of the road that seemed still attached through an invisible car to her resisting body. The wedding dress was heavy.

Papa B appeared not to notice it at all. "I came in through the basement door," he said, as if that confession must set to rest the only question that might arise about his presence.

She was desperately silent.

"I hit it with my shoulder and it opened. The basement door. Sort of rotten. I've nailed it shut, don't worry." He touched his right shoulder. "Hurt myself a bit."

Then he went on shaping the figure he held in his left hand by cutting it, trimming it, with the scissors.

He'd nailed himself in. Don't worry, he said. We're nailed in here together. And he was sitting there at her desk as if he owned it. His tall black hat loomed and threatened on the desk beside her typewriter and her disorder of notes and guesses, her failed attempts at telling herself her mislaid story, her cryptic wonderings at her own reasons for believing anyone had a first chance, let alone a second one.

And still she was silent. The silence only assured the man at her desk, the man occupying her chair and her warm cocoon of light, there in that attic full of darkness.

"Ah," he said. Perhaps he could make out, in the gloom beyond his lamp, the hint of an expression on Maggie's face. "They're after me, you know."

She wouldn't do it. She refused. She wouldn't cry out, in sympathy and wonder, *Who's* after you? He sat there pathetic with all his male need bleating to her. She refused to offer him a single word.

She turned and went down the steps. She didn't stop on the second floor, she went carefully down the stairs to the main floor, carefully in her wedding dress made the turn, went to the kitchen. She was, she told herself, going to make herself a cup of coffee. And then, about to reach for a filter, she found the full cup of coffee in her hand.

He is up there, I saw him. I am not simply exhausted, hallucinating, I saw him there in his untrimmed face and that wigwam of a cassock or whatever it is he wears instead of decent clothing.

Then she went, cautiously, to the front door. *They,* after all, were after him. She checked the lock. She looked at the grandfather clock and couldn't make any sense of its hands or of its meticulous ticking. She returned to the kitchen, found the coffee tin, the filters. That finding seemed to require a long and careful search, a remarkable show of persistence, a will to make heroic discoveries. She set water to boil on the stove, disliking her ever-invisible cousin again for his not owning an electric kettle. She lifted down from an open shelf an empty coffee mug.

Carefully, evasively, she wiped the cup clean with a dish towel.

She could go outside and get into Bludgett's car and go to the police station. If first she changed clothes. She could go to see Bludgett, wake him up from his sleeplessness, on bended knees ask him to come running. She could catch Ida and Josie getting ready for bed and ask for the rye and ginger she'd refused and while gulping it down suggest they all go racing back to the controlled insanities of Deadman Spring.

She could, more easily than anything else, go up to her bedroom and get the bag that she hadn't quite ever unpacked on her trip to Deadman Spring. She could drive to the airport, park the car, buy a ticket on a credit card, catch the next flight to Greece.

Each step of the attic stairway was a cliff strewn with granite rubble and jagged scree and shattered ice. Far above, something terrible was happening. Had happened. Would happen.

Maggie set the mug of coffee on the desk in front of Papa B. Or Vasilis. Or Billy. Or Dorfendorf. Or whatever the hell his name was, assuming he had a name of his own. She kept her mug of cold coffee for herself and went and sat on the old brown leather sofa behind her chair, in the dormer window. Papa B didn't turn around. She spoke to the knot of hair at the back of her head.

"Okay. I can't resist. I'll ask the question, so you can get on with the answer you've got planned in that thick head of yours. *Who* is after you?"

"How was the trip?" Papa B said.

He reminded her of Henry. He reminded her of her cousin George, gone out of sight on the day they were scheduled to meet. He reminded her of Tom Bludgett.

"Fine." she savoured that monosyllabic answer, leaving it to ring empty and meaningless in the ears that were to be found, supposedly, under that mop of curly, greying hair. Then she couldn't resist adding,

"Just perfect. Couldn't have been better. And I'm delighted that your friend Bludgett kept you informed of my whereabouts."

Papa B put down his scissors and turned slowly on the chair, as if afraid he might, moving, lose his balance and topple to the floor. Or spill the coffee he was picking up while he turned.

"The cat's out of the bag," he said. "I'm out in the open."

Good grief, she thought, good God, the man is a criminal, a murderer, a fugitive, a fake priest, a man in a woman's dress cutting out paper dolls — and now on top of all that he wants to be mothered and held.

"You're hardly out in the open." Maggie gestured helplessly at the dark corners of the attic.

He was deaf as a post. He heard nothing she said. "It seems," he said, "that somebody went up to Deadman Spring and spilled the beans."

Maggie sipped her coffee. "Well don't blame Ida or Josie or me. That guy Fish seemed to be expecting us."

"He *was* expecting you. Inez called him to say you were on the way."

"Inez Catonio knew?"

"Half the goddamned country knew you were going on a trip to Deadman Spring to look for a missing corpse."

"You sound like me," Maggie said. 'You're exaggerating. Ida and Josie knew. Bludgett knew. How did Inez know?"

"Ida told her. She had to ask for time off, didn't she? Ida doesn't skip the reasons why or lack for opinions."

"Good for Ida."

"Inez phoned Deadman Spring the morning you left. She got Fish on the phone."

"That must have been an exercise in futility."

"She told him you're some kind of schemer who sits around in a wedding dress trying to figure out who killed that famous spa doctor up on Kootenay Lake."

"And I trust she explained that she had you, the murderer, prisoner in her house."

"Nothing that blatant, Maggie. She simply told him she knew where to find me."

"She was going to turn you over to Deemer! For cash on the barrelhead, I suppose."

"Hold on, Maggie. No, not quite. She just thought I'd have to stay — You know. Where could I go, after word was out?"

"Then why in hell did you come *here*?"

"Because you're looking for me too. You're trying to hunt me down." Papa B was mightily pleased with his logic. "No one is going to look for me here. Get it?"

Maggie thought of her calendars. She wanted to run down to the kitchen and check all four at once, as if some averaging of dates might fix for her not only the day but also the moment of her disaster. Where and when had she made her wrong move? Had an ancestor somewhere in the past erred, and left her condemned to try blindly to make the accidental gesture that would set things right? She would become a collector of wristwatches, of sundials. She would scour the world, if she survived this, for ways to turn the clock back five minutes.

"Who knows where you are?" Maggie said.

"Nobody. I parked my pizza car at the airport and came here on foot with half a dozen cassettes that would give me away and a ring of keys and a small pizza that someone must still be waiting for. It was the middle of the night and pouring rain. When I got here I ate the pizza."

"You don't like pizza," she said. She added to herself, absurdly, hating herself for thinking it, he can wear some of George's clothes. Half the drawers in the bedroom are full of shorts and socks, my cousin must have a fetish. The closets are full of expensive denim shirts. And then she thought, but how to get this man into a clean shirt?

"You'll have to leave," Maggie said. "If you just simply leave, I won't call the cops."

"The cops have been looking for me for four years. That De Medeiros business."

Business. He had the nerve to call it business, a matter that might be settled over a pub lunch. An exchange of correspondence. A telephone call or two — yes, poor fellow, seems to have killed someone in a fit of jealousy over a woman who was dead.

"And I won't call Jack Deemer. Just you leave. Get up off that chair. Stand up. Walk. Leave. Depart. Vamoose. Skidaddle. Just vanish." She paused. "But I might tell Inez."

Papa B made a motion as if in trying to get up he found he was glued to the chair. "I can't just go out there —"

"No, of course not." Maggie caught herself sipping her coffee in his dumb, melancholy way. "You had the whole damned city to hide in. Go back to Mount Athos."

And then it struck her, watching him there, as he let his face go blank. She'd seen his picture in a newspaper in the Canadian Embassy in Athens. She and Henry had had a wild argument, because she wanted to photograph the picture that was in the paper. I was like Karen Strike, Maggie thought. Henry and I quarrelled because I wanted to take a photograph of a newspaper picture of a face. "Why photograph it?" Henry said. "Just steal the goddamned thing." "I want a photograph," I said, "not the clipping." "Fine," Henry said. "Fine. Have it your way. I'll take a photograph for you." And that because he had taken inadequate photographs of hundreds of icons in badly lit and crowded churches and chapels. He believed the function of a chapel was to enable him to view icons. They were quarrelling bitterly, after days of being extremely polite to each other while he led her from village to town, from one small hotel room to another, from one altar screen to another. The picture in the newspaper there in Athens was simply a man's head, in black and white. The man was believed to be in Greece and was involved in the death of a famous spa doctor. There was something in the story about a disappearance. But the spa doctor was the real news, not the man whose face was in the newspaper. All she wanted was a snapshot of the picture of the beardless man; it would fit into a story she was drafting. "'The Imposter,'" Henry said, when she asked if she could use his camera. Henry hated criminals, especially criminals who got themselves into trouble. "Call it 'The Imposter.' It's your kind of story." That was Henry. He hated her writing with a concentration that was the most delicate accomplishment of his life. "The face," Maggie said, "is drained of all existence." "The way you think yours is," Henry said. She had entered the Embassy simply to read a few newspapers from the city that had once been her home. "'The Poseur,'" Henry said, holding his camera out of her reach. "Look at him. He's totally guilty. Look. His face is his confession."

Maggie said nothing now, of the picture, to the bearded man in her chair. "Excuse me," she said. "I have to go pee."

And that same day, there in Athens, was the day she knew she would one day go back to Vancouver. She began to plot. She wrote, in a small frenzy of hope and resignation, the book of stories she'd been telling herself for ten years that she was going to write. She remembered, while writing the last page of the last story in the book, the wedding dress she had put away in her cousin's attic and forgotten.

She set her mug on the desk and hurried to the stairway and went down the steep steps, then along the hallway to the bathroom. We'll have to share a bathroom, she realized, sitting down, these damned old houses with one toilet, and that on the second floor.

She ripped at the toilet paper, she dabbed between her thighs. She didn't need a man in the house, she'd fled all the way across the continent to escape the dependencies and resentments of Henry Ketch, she wanted to be alone, whatever the pain. And the pleasures were merciless and beautiful. The first gift of all was her cousin's vanishing, his disappearing into a rain forest on the other side of the globe. You're on your own, love. Find it.

Downstairs in the kitchen, the phone was ringing. It had to be Bludgett, there was no way to phone him; the idiot didn't believe in phones, they'd wake him out of the sleep he was pretending not to have. But he'd go to a pay phone and phone anyone he knew at any time of the day or night. She hurried, trying not to break her neck on the stairs, and that was another male trick, her cousin's this time, one phone in a three-story house, you can only talk on one phone, he'd said over the phone, before he left, before she arrived.

"Hello?"

"Maggie?"

"Yes."

"Maggie, has Inez called you?"

Maggie felt her stomach tumble. "What?"

"I gave her your number."

"Ida! Honestly."

"She just phoned me. She's on the rampage. Papa B has disappeared."

Maggie tried to find a way to sound surprised and couldn't. "Great," she said. "Grand." She wanted to scream into the telephone receiver. But why scream at Ida? We are always, she thought, screaming at the wrong person.

"Right into thin air. Gone. Vanished."

"Perfect," Maggie said. If only, she thought — if only he was gone and vanished. Or maybe he wasn't up there in the attic. "Fabulous. Just great. A good riddance."

"Maggie!"

"I'm sorry."

"She thinks Deemer got him. She's called in the police."

"Heaven help us, Ida. The police. What police? Thirty-seven varieties of police have been looking for him for four years. What makes her think they'll find him now?"

"She told them he works for her. Out of Midnight Pizza. What if he shows up there? Or what if he goes back to Inez's house?"

At least, Maggie thought, at least up until now he was self-supporting. Now he can't even go to work. "What's wrong with Inez?"

"I'm going to call Fish," Ida said. "Right now. I'm going to warn him that Inez Catonio has the police looking for Papa B and wants him back, dead or alive."

"But why?"

"But why, what?"

"Why does she want him back? That badly?"

"Why?" Ida was baffled by the question. "Good grief, Maggie. Haven't you noticed? She's in love with him."

She went upstairs with two tuna sandwiches, two empty tumblers, and a pitcher of milk on a tray. It's come to this, she thought. Again. The last one claimed he was so busy he couldn't join me for a meal, but he never got a word of his study written. Now I'm making sandwiches for a man who's cutting out dolls.

"Who was it?" Papa B said. "I thought I heard the phone."

"I think you did. It was your Aunt Ida. And why didn't you go running to your Aunt Ida's?"

She remembered Ida saying, but they haven't come up with a corpse. No stiff, no murderer. She would oblige. She would pack him into one of George's specimen boxes, call Purolator.

"Did you hear me?"

"Think, Maggie. What's the first place they'll start watching, after they question Elizabeth?" He took half a sandwich in either hand. Maggie was embarrassed by his hunger. He was eating and mumbling: "Maybe I'll head back to Greece. If I can borrow some money."

"Look up my husband while you're at it. You two would make a great pair. If you're so eager to get back to Mount Athos" — she heard her voice, my God, I'm trying to keep him from leaving — "why did you come back here to begin with?" And before he could answer, she added, "And by the way, how much money *do* you have?"

"I have thirty-nine dollars and seventy-two cents." And then he answered the question she had tried to stop him from answering. "We — most of us — want to have another shot at it. If you'll pardon the pun. Don't we?"

"You'll need some blankets."

"I used one of those rugs." He indicated one of the small oriental rugs. "Got here late at night. Made myself at home."

She ignored that too. "You'll need a quilt and some sheets. This place can be like an icebox. That's why I keep that electric heater there by the desk. By my desk."

"I used it to take the chill off. Raided the fridge first. Had to get up here in a hurry." He was talking and eating. "Can't go back to the kitchen. Bathroom, yes. But that's the limit." He was pushing food into his mouth while he chewed. "Anyone could see in through a ground-floor window, the way this house is designed. Can't be too careful."

Now he had the gall to talk about being careful. "You'll need a pillow. A real pillow." She poked at a pillow at one end of the sofa. "This thing is like a bag of rocks."

"I was just hanging in."

On top of everything else, he saw himself as a hero. She moved her sandwich out of his reach.

"A hot plate," she said. "You'll need a hot plate, I saw one in the basement. Maybe you noticed it — while you were looking for nails and a hammer." She was pleased with that little dig. "Thanks, at least, for letting *me* back in." She looked around the attic. "You can keep the milk cool in the far window." She pointed. "For a day or two. While you plot your escape. I'm not your servant."

"I'm sorry," he said.

"*Sorry.* You're *sorry.* Listen, B — or Dorf. You haven't even got a name I can get hold of. And here you are —" She piled her notes and files and a box of paper onto her typewriter. "I'll work at my kitchen table tomorrow. You stay put." She was leaving. She stopped on the steps, her hands full, her head level with the attic floor. "Use the bathroom, okay. But never ever come down to the first floor. Never. And hand me that pen, would you? The green one."

He stood up from the desk; he picked up the pen. Her hands were full. He stooped and set the pen into her mouth.

"And do some serious thinking," she said, her pen in her teeth.

8

On the morning of her third day home from Deadman Spring Maggie decided the time had come, she must give Papa B an ultimatum, he had to announce his plans and the date of his intended departure.

She searched the kitchen cupboards and found a pack of cigarettes, then hid them again, in a casserole this time. She clung to the sheer sanity of the fridge clicking on, clicking off, the furnace coming on in the basement, while she pretended to work.

The wedding dress was in the musty closet in her bedroom, with George's two tweed suits and his denim shirts and his gaudy ties. She couldn't bring herself so much as to look at the dress, let alone put it on. Not with Papa B in the house.

She made grocery lists. Not daring to call Midnight Pizza for deliveries, she had to go shopping. Two people, for some reason, ate four times as much as one. She would go to a store and start to pick up the items on her list. Then she would decide that someone was watching, wondering why one person needed so much food. Or she would wonder if she had locked the door; Bludgett or Ida or Josie might drop by, and, not getting an answer, become worried and try the knob, walk into the house, start calling her name, start climbing the stairs. Then she would pick four of five items out of her cart, hurry to the express line, hurry home to her locked door.

Flee to Greece all right. Except that his thirty-nine dollars and seventy-two cents wouldn't get him past the airport cafeteria.

Maggie made fresh coffee. Now that she had given up cigarettes she was on her way to a caffeine addiction. At least she was kicking the pizza habit. The coffee would be her excuse, she would take it up to the attic, settle down on the sofa, get a conversation going with that impossible man, broach the apparently unanswerable question. Just when the hell are you leaving?

The phone was trying to catch the neighbourhood's attention. Maggie leapt to the wall and snatched the receiver.

It was Bludgett. He was speaking before she answered.

"Maggie?" he said again.

"Yes," she said. "Yes, yes, yes."

"I can't hear what you're saying."

"I'm not saying anything. I'm practising to be a monk." She wanted to kick herself for mentioning monks, that would tell Bludgett what was on her mind.

"You need more sex."

"Around you, less is more."

"Did you sell my car? I've been worried about you."

She sat down at the kitchen table beside the tray and the coffee mugs and her typewriter. "Damn. I forgot."

"Maggie. You couldn't just *forget* that you borrowed someone's car."

"I swear. I forgot."

"Thank you. Remind me not to lend you a million dollars."

"Thomas, don't take it personally —"

"Listen, I'm joking. I'll drop right over and pick it up myself."

"No. Please, Thomas. I'm working. I don't mean you shouldn't come over. I mean, not right now. In a day or two. I'll deliver it right away."

"You're spending too much time alone, Maggie."

"Not enough. I'm busy as a bee."

Maggie was certain she heard hammering in the attic. Perhaps the idiot up there was trying to get out by smashing a hole through the roof. Why not the basement door again, that was broken already.

"Okay," Bludgett said. "This is it, work or no work. You and I go to dinner with Inez Catonio. Tomorrow night."

"Why, Thomas? I don't think I can make it."

"Inez is at her wit's end. We have to help out."

" — — "

"She's at her wit's end, Maggie."

"I heard you."

"I trust you've heard about Papa B. Ida says she told you."

"She told me."

"You don't seem terribly concerned."

"Thomas, I'm concerned. Okay? Believe me. I'm concerned."

"We're taking Inez to dinner. Seven-thirty sharp. Just to hold her hand if nothing else."

Maggie had to get off the phone. Tomorrow night. That was the deadline. She'd have her attic empty by then, her life in order. Maybe she'd just imagined the hammering, it was her own attempt at breaking out of her own disaster. "If you had a phone of your own, I'd say I'll call you back."

"It's settled. I'll come by to pick up the car. We'll take it from there."

"Thomas, listen. I'll pick you up. Tomorrow night. Seven on the button. Why should you come by here when it's easier for me to drive over there?"

"I'll walk. I need the exercise."

She pretended not to have heard. "Seven-fifteen. I'll be waiting outside your apartment. You might recognize the car. It's a rusted blue Pontiac that shouldn't be on the road."

Papa B didn't notice her breathlessness. "You see," he said, waving his sleeves around at the attic walls, "with the windows sealed, I can work with the shadow puppets any time of the day or night." He had opened a bale of botanical specimens; he had taken off the clamps and pulled out the sheets of wood and used them to seal tight the windows. "Now we're getting ready for action."

Maggie set down the coffee tray on the desk beside the figure of a puppet and sank onto the sofa. "Action," she said. "Okay. Tell George about it. Shoot."

Papa B gently touched the outline on the desk. He had constructed a cardboard pattern about the height of his raised forearm and hand — the figure of a man with two moveable legs and a moveable right arm. Half of the face was nose. The right eye had not yet been put into the blank space cut into the profiled head. The large feet were bare, with spaces cut into the cardboard for toenails. When Papa B held up the figure, the long right arm, hinged in three places, swung below the figure's knees.

"After I failed as a logger —" Papa B stuck the eraser end of a pencil into a socket on the back of the figure. "There on Mount Athos. . . . I was put to work cleaning up old books. Illuminated manuscripts. Icons. You name it. That's what my training was. I once worked in a museum, before I hired on with Jack Deemer. But the two old monks in charge, they preferred shadow puppets to saints." He rolled the pencil between two fingers; he swung the empty outline, setting the limbs into motion. "On the sly they had their puppet shows. They sent me out to find paint and leather, bigger candles. I was a foreigner. I was somehow exempt from reprisal, they liked to believe. I could do the scrounging."

He put down the outline on the desk again. He was rhapsodic, describing what he'd need: cellophane, some tubes of paint, more cardboard, wire, needles, thread, a smaller hammer, a better pair of pliers. He rummaged in the mess on Maggie's desk to find his list.

"Different colours of cellophane," he said. "You choose. I'll cut the figures out of cardboard — like this one. Unless you find some cheap leather. That would be better. More durable. Once I've got the figures in outline, see, I cut holes in them. I set in the cellophane." He bent to his shopping list and wrote in a correction. "Just get plain cellophane. The heavy kind. I'll paint it myself. Or you can help. The light will shine through from behind." And again he was going over his list. "I almost forgot. I need a radio that will play tapes." He indicated two cassettes on the desk.

She was trying to find a space in his talk for her argument. Instead she said, "There's a radio in the living room, sitting on that TV set that doesn't work. It should play tapes."

"And a bed sheet," he said. "Just an ordinary bed sheet. White. We can stretch it tight on the frame I'm building." He indicated a corner of the attic where he'd taken apart two of George's crates. He gave Maggie no space for her questions. "Rods. Some of those thin curtain rods, the old kind, there must be a whole bundle somewhere down in the basement. I mount the puppets on the ends of rods. It's simple. You're the audience. I hold the flat puppets against the screen — against the stretched sheet." He picked up the outline again. "See? Imagine the screen is between us. The room is dark. I turn on a bright light here behind the screen. You'll have to get me a better light. Then I hold the shadow puppet to the screen."

Papa B was delighted with himself. "All the way from China to Turkey. Caravans. The Silk Route. They're from the Orient, the shadow puppets. They got traded west." He held the outlined figure away from himself so that he might become the audience. "It was the Greeks, under the tyranny of the Turks — the Greeks figured out how to let the puppets say what couldn't be said."

"Henry hates the shadow puppet shows."

"You've seen them? You saw them when you were in Greece?"

"Never. Henry wouldn't so much as stick his head into a puppeteer's tent. He likes his pictures to stand still."

"Too bad he can't join us. We could invite him to our show."

"Our show? Listen, Papa B —"

She was on her way down the stairs. He was calling after her. She'd forgotten his list. She must hurry, she had laundry to do. He was calling, but he was stopped at the top of the attic stairs, by a wonderful, invisible barrier. She had to clear him out, that was obvious, he would never arrange anything himself. She must clean up the place, it was starting to look like a pigsty. She must get some letters written, some phone calls made.

Just the facts, please, she typed. I'm okay. She was at the kitchen table. This very evening I'm going out for dinner, hurray, I'm going out for dinner, I'm getting out of this house, hurray, hurray, I'm having dinner with Thomas Bludgett, I'll go pick him up in his car, Thomas and I are having dinner with Inez Catonio, just the facts please, Inez Catonio. Papa B delivers pizza from one of Inez Catonio's pizza joints. He used to. He wants to. He used to want to.

No, Maggie typed. *Obiter*. What's the phrase that Bludgett likes to throw at her? *Obiter dicta*.

What are you really waiting for, Maggie Wilder?

I should run upstairs, she typed, and take a shower, get ready for my first night out since Papa B nailed shut the basement door. Fucking coffin. I'll be here forever, she typed. I have to do his laundry, he doesn't dare venture onto the main floor, let alone into the basement; but they aren't his clothes to begin with, they're George's shorts and socks, George's pyjamas. I wanted him to try on George's shirts and trousers; instead he wears pyjamas when he isn't in his fake cassock. I don't dare wash it, it would dissolve.

She stopped typing and listened. The machine in the basement went on with its sucky, obscene rhythm. She had to wait for clean clothes for her night out. Nothing would ever stop. Josie would go on forever making wedding dresses, inventing brides by making wedding dresses to be cleaned and sealed in plastic and stored in closets and attics. Ida, answering the phone in Midnight Pizza, dispatching blistering circles of pizza into the bottomless gut —

He'd be up there forever. Papa B. In her attic. Jack Deemer had guessed right, the world had become an attic. So rummage.

She listened again for the washing machine to stop. The kitchen was quiet, except for the clock in the hallway. The calendars seemed safely asleep, folded over themselves. She had, to avoid the attic, to avoid thinking, done all the dishes, set the kitchen slick and clean, put away the ironing board.

Henry was right too. Live within boundaries. He refused to go to the USSR or Turkey or Yugoslavia. He refused to think about the icons of Novgorod, of Pskov, of Kiev, of Bulgarian villages, of Turkish museums. Let them be part of the attic that remained unexplored. He would concentrate on the icons of one small patch of the Byzantine world, a peninsula and a handful of islands organized by the Aegean. Maggie, grudgingly, admired that about Henry, even if she couldn't understand. The Aegean too was icon, for him.

The washing machine had stopped. She would run the dryer. Then it would be time to shout up the attic stairway, to holler, victorious, up to Papa B: I'm going out. I'm going to have dinner with Bludgett and Inez. I'm going to tell them where you are.

They were eating linguine pescatore, she and Inez and Bludgett. The restaurant was white inside, the walls, the tablecloths, the dishes. The tiled floor was white. The roses on the tables, the hanging ferns, gave colour to the room. But the room was a stark white, and the white turned the dark in the frames of the windows into a polished, contained dark. The windows were luminous pictures of an outside that Maggie was beginning to forget, in her days and nights with Papa B.

Inez was wearing black. Her necklace was thickly gold, her bracelets gold. The dark of her hair was a frame on the ivory whiteness of her face. She had the air about her of someone trying to carry on a conversation while listening for a telephone to ring.

They were drinking wine. "Thomas and I," Inez said, "tried to be lovers. We were a dismal failure. Did you tell Maggie about our dismal failure, Thomas?"

Bludgett nodded, but said, no, he hadn't. He was wearing a black leather tie with the same plaid shirt he'd been wearing when Maggie had last seen him. Or had first seen him.

"I like men who are failures," Inez said, "but Thomas overdoes it. Really. He overdoes it." Inez touched the back of Maggie's left hand. "Don't you think, Maggie, our friend Thomas overdoes failure?"

Catonio. That was her husband's name. She explained to Maggie. They were drinking wine. Her mention of failures made her think again of her former husband. Her family was partly Spanish and Mexican, one of the outfits that ran huge herds in the Interior. She had grown up a cowgirl. Then she married a man in Kamloops who was trying to make a living selling pizza. And then, somehow, somewhere, watching her husband fail, she decided it would be a lot more fun running a pizza empire and succeeding than running cattle in a semi-desert and sometimes succeeding and sometimes failing. She arrived unannounced in Vancouver and bought a string of pizza places. And succeeded.

"The past," Inez said, "was gone from my life. Vanished. Leave that to the likes of Jack Deemer."

Bludgett sipped his wine. "The past has a way of presenting itself as success. No wonder you hate it."

She was listening for a telephone to ring. "I like pizza. The pizza version of present. Thomas, you order pizza without thinking about the beauty of it all. That's where you fail. You don't know how to make the present present."

"Perhaps I should succeed. Just to spite you."

She shook her bracelets back and put her right thumb to her left wrist. "Perhaps you should take your own pulse. Try. Or don't you want to take the risk? Perhaps you're a ghost."

"That's why you need Papa B, isn't it?" Bludgett was pouring wine. "He's a way of taking your own pulse."

"You've got it. He's even better than masturbation. And that's expecting a lot of a man."

"What's going to happen if we don't find him?"

"He isn't like you," Inez said. "He doesn't lock himself in when he goes to take a pee."

"You aren't answering my question."

"I learned long ago never to answer your questions." Inez turned to Maggie, ignoring Bludgett. "When Papa B showed up — his aunt brought him by. Ida is a friend. Years ago she worked for my mother, feeding ranch hands. I gave Papa B a job because Ida said he needed one."

"He also needed a place to stay," Bludgett said. "Apparently."

"You were never there when I needed you. Were you, Thomas?"

"I take it Papa B is."

Inez stabbed at a scallop and raised it to her mouth, then put it down. She took another sip of wine.

"When I get hold of that man I'm going to feed him prairie oyster pizza. And the prairie oysters will be his own. Tell him that — since I assume he's hiding out in your filthy apartment."

"I'd be too incompetent to hide anyone. And besides, your private detective watches my place so closely I'm soon going to charge him with obstructing the view."

"My wonderful private detective couldn't find his own ass if he was looking for it with both hands."

"At least he's methodical. I know exactly when his itinerary will bring him to my street."

"So far he's discovered that you buy milk, puffed rice, and a lot of pizzas. And you leave your light on at night."

"He has the capacity for failure that you admire in men."

"He's not my kind of failure. Mr Hasegawa believes he's succeeding. I like men who know exactly that they're failing and why and how. You are, Thomas, in spite of everything, an awfully attractive man."

Inez had a private detective at work, along with the police, and Maggie, instead of inquiring further, wanted only to ask a domestic question. She had gone to a lot of trouble to find a few things for Papa B; he had thanked her by coming up with a revised list. Where, she wanted to ask, can I find good art supplies at prices I can afford?

"What if you don't find him?" Maggie asked. "What if he isn't hiding in Thomas's apartment?"

"I'll find him. And when I do I'm going to phone Jack Deemer and tell him I've got a collection I want to sell. A collection of collections. One hundred and twenty-four weak excuses. Portions of a tongue. Eighty-two reasons why up and down are the same thing. Six explanations of why stupid is smart, and vice versa. Two testicles that might compose a pair." Inez raised her wineglass to Bludgett. "At least you could never be broken down into a collection of anything."

"Consider the dead god," Bludgett said, raising his own glass to the hanging ferns, "his parts various cast upon the flowing waters. I hear regret in your voice. And what part do you intend to keep?"

"The part you so dearly like to keep to yourself, Thomas. And I hear jealousy in your voice. And don't pretend you aren't hiding him."

Inez turned and signalled a waiter. "Christopher. Bring us the dessert menu, would you?" And then to Maggie: "Let's you and I have dessert. And cognac. Thomas can finish that inadequate wine he ordered on his own."

She had a way of pursing her lips after she spoke; no matter what she said, she proceeded after to offer a kiss.

Is not each pizza, fresh out of an oven, set on a table and sliced, an icon speaking at least one of our basic needs? I have never in my whole long life so much as touched a finger to a pizza, and yet I grant the pizza queen her small victories. The rubble and design of a pizza, its ordered blur of colours and textures and shapes, arouse in me the collector's will to win.

Inez Catonio, as I was shortly to hear from the detective she employed, fancied herself quite a looker. Mr Hasegawa was a small, deliberate man, not given to exaggeration. He knew all kinds of irrelevant things about Inez Catonio, and nothing about Papa B. He knew, for instance, that Inez Catonio did not have about her all the generosity that her blowing of kisses hither and yon might suggest.

The photograph of Maggie Wilder, on the other hand, was quite a different matter.

Let me explain in parenthesis that I, Jack Deemer, received the photographs from Karen Strike by courier the day after she took them. That was the first glimpse I had of Maggie. In one photograph she lifts herself naked out of the water, into the caress of snowflakes. Perhaps it was right then, examining that photograph, that I became interested in the icon, though I had not yet heard of Maggie's husband nor of his obsession. The little patch of sight that remains mine turned the snapshot iconic. Is not each treasured snowflake itself a kind of icon?

I studied that one particular photograph. There, that February afternoon in Calgary, sitting alone in the office in one of my cavernous and stuffed warehouses, I was smitten. It had nothing at all to do with the dress that Karen, quoting Fish, made mention of in her covering note.

I carry the photograph in my briefcase. In the large black-and-white photograph, Maggie's mouth is full and open, her breasts small, her stomach pulled into an exquisite, tight circle around her wet belly button as she raises her long arms in an offered embrace. The air is full of unhappy ghosts and hesitating promises. Fish is not in the photograph at all.

9

It was after midnight when Maggie went up the stairs toward her bedroom. She would go straight to bed, she was too exhausted to deal with Papa B, let him sulk in his marooned ark with the sound of rain drumming in his ears. And she was angry at herself, for saying too much, for hardly talking at all.

Maggie was in the bathroom, raising a tissue to her eyes, when she heard the music. It came from the attic. Strident. Aggressive.

And then the voice came up behind the strange, familiar music. "Oh-pa, oh-pa." And again, "Oh-pa, oh-pa."

The sudden voice was not Papa B's, it was Greek, calling upon the audience to take heed. "Yah-soo. Yah-soo," it added. "Yah-soo."

Maggie went slowly up the attic stairs. She would tell Papa B of Inez and how, in spite of everything, she liked the woman. Somehow, she was on Inez's side, it was better to risk everything yourself rather than having someone do it for you. "You mean," Maggie had asked over chocolate cake, "close your eyes and leap?" Inez didn't hesitate. She was having raspberry mousse. "Open your eyes and leap," she said.

The attic was dark.

And then the tape stopped playing.

Maggie was about to turn back down the stairs when a light came on. She went up the last few steps.

The light was behind a screen at the far end of the attic. Papa B had mounted a bed sheet inside a large frame. The light made of the white sheet a blank space, an empty window. A frame without a picture.

A figure peeked in on the left side of the screen. Then disappeared again.

A house came onto the screen on Maggie's right. It remained there. The black outline of the house was filled with cellophane patches: a green attic, two levels of rooms, one orange, one brown, two purple flights of stairs.

The puppet reappeared on the left. Karaghiosi. It was Karaghiosi, the most popular of all the Greek shadow puppets. He swaggered across the screen. He was dressed in traditional Greek dress, a skirted man, a short and hunchbacked and bald-headed man with a low forehead, a huge and bulbous nose and feet to match, a long and hinged right arm that dangled below his knees. The patches of painted cellophane, in red and blue and yellow, were set like stained glass into the black frame of his body.

"Hello. Hello. Maggie Wilder? Are you in there?" It was Karaghiosi speaking, guttural, cantankerous. Standing outside the door, he knocked again with his long, hinged right arm. "Are you locked in there, Maggie Wilder? Do you want out?"

"I'm not at home to you," a voice answered. "Leave me alone."

There was no figure to be seen inside the house, only a voice to be heard. Papa B was speaking both voices, but neither was his. The voice of the second and invisible speaker, Maggie recognized, was an imitation of her own.

She sat down on the sofa. She'd had too much wine, she was uncertain of how to respond. Papa B was invisible behind the screen, standing back of the light. Maggie saw the shadows of two rods playing faintly on the screen. Karaghiosi bent forward and knocked at the door with his head.

"Go away," the voice said from inside the house.

"Do you want out, Maggie Wilder?"

"No, I do not," Maggie's voice answered.

"Do you want me to join you in there, Maggie Wilder?"

"Never, never, never. I want to be alone."

The voice of Karaghiosi was coarse, mocking. "Then why don't you tell me to stop knocking?"

Maggie moved from the sofa and sat at her desk. She couldn't resist, she broke in and said, "Karaghiosi, you are always pretending to be someone you aren't. I know that much about you. You're pretending to be Papa B."

Karaghiosi pounded again with his right arm at the door of the house on the screen. "Let me out," he shouted, from outside the house. "Get me out of here."

Maggie got up from her desk and went to the house on the screen. She pretended to knock.

"Come in." The voice that spoke was the voice that pretended to be Maggie's.

Maggie stopped knocking. "Please," she said. "Please, Maggie, let him in."

Karaghiosi hooted with laughter. He retreated from the house on the screen and was gone. In a moment he returned, carrying an enormous pizza.

Papa B spoke in Maggie's voice. "Now where is Inez? The pizza is here and Inez is nowhere in sight."

Maggie, watching Karaghiosi's consternation, knocked again at the door where he waited.

The voice of Maggie spoke again. "Join us. Please do join us, Inez."

Maggie was shocked and yet excited too, by the name she was given. She had become part of the play. She liked that. Karaghiosi did not enter the house, he spoke as if speaking at once to the woman inside the house and to the woman outside.

"Try it," Karaghiosi said. "Shrimp and black olive and artichoke heart. You'll like it."

"No," Maggie said. The voice of the Maggie in the house.

Karaghiosi disappeared from the screen. He returned with two large pizzas balanced teetering on his raised hand. "Eggplant and slices of ginger." He knocked violently at the door of the house with his head. "It's me, Maggie." He balanced the two pizzas wildly on the hand of his long right arm. "Inez and I are freezing out here in the rain. Please, Maggie."

Maggie reached out as if to catch the teetering stack of pizzas. "Yes," she said.

"Thank you," Karaghiosi said. "Thank you, Inez."

The voice of Maggie, in the house, told Karaghiosi to enter.

"I can't," Karaghiosi answered. "I'm with Inez."

Maggie touched a hand to the bed sheet that was the screen. A hand touched hers in response. She felt the hand finding hers and pressed against it and tried to speak. She knew she could not, try as she might, imitate Inez's voice; she said nothing. But she pressed her hand to the screen. She went on pressing her hand against the hand that responded and she knew she had entered into the house on the screen, she was inside and somewhere on the first floor, then on the second, finding the flight of purple stairs that would take her to the attic.

The light went off behind the screen. But the voice of Karaghiosi went on, addressing Inez. It did nothing more than offer a list. Papaya. Bacon. Green pepper. The voice swam softly in the darkness. Smoked oysters. Onions. Salami. Feta. The attic was pitch dark. The floating hands attached themselves to bodies. The floating words attached themselves to tongues.

Maggie hesitated, waiting for my response; I begged her to continue. And yet she had nothing to tell me that I could not have guessed, for in the years while I was living with Julie Magnuson I learned that disguise is a prod to desire. She needed pretence, and I was never the pretender she would have. I was only my blunt and honest self. Other men satisfied her. Manny De Medeiros, the scheming little doctor, pretending to be the great healer. My own purchasing agent, William Dorfendorf, pretending to scour the world on my behalf, looking for a perfect spa, while he tended to his own brute needs. They met in Portugal, the two men together with Julie; they pretended the spa in Luso was the spa that would bring me health and renewal. I got that much out of De Medeiros before Dorf fired his fateful shot. De Medeiros spoke, and I felt no jealousy. I was pleased that he let me hear from his own red lips of Julie's too brief happiness, the three of them, she and Manny and Dorf, there in Portugal, away from the sad constraints of home, sharing their lives, sharing one voluptuous bed.

Maggie, I suspect, felt that in telling me the story of her love affair with puppets was telling me back into my own desire. And in a way she was. Listening, I was aroused and made as willing as I had been, back then, by De Medeiros and his anxious tale. We sat in the cave at Deadman Spring, he and Dorf and I; we sat together naked on a rock shelf in the hot mineral water in the cave, and I was at once audience and priest while they confessed their abandon. They had got into one sweet bed together, Julie and her two lovers. Manny De Medeiros, her dwarf and philosopher and healer. Dorf, her animal and saintly man. She, Julie, had there for her few brief days, received all that she imagined receiving, given what she would give. All that. And waters to heal their exhaustion.

I am a collector. Perhaps to collect is to have all and nothing. It is to heap ashes on one's own head. It is to desire all and to embrace the emptiness. Maggie Wilder, in her teasing way, came to my rescue.

She did not, the second night after her first, go up to the attic until she heard the music and the call. "Oh-pa. Oh-pa. Yah-soo." She did not go up the stairs until a faint glow from the farther end of the attic told her the performance was about to begin, and she was again to be a sterling part of that performance.

I know about performances. They were helpless with each other, all day, Maggie and Dorf. They ignored each other and worse. Their silences were surly. And viciously animal. I know, I know well, those strategies of avoidance and attraction. Julie Magnuson in her desire was as sudden as a whip.

Maggie went up the stairs and a new figure was on the screen. The puppet on the screen was monk-like in his dress, wearing a tall black hat with straight sides, a flat top. He stood, his arms at his sides, his hands empty, in front of the house that stood now at the centre of the screen. He was humble. He beseeched.

He reached up to take off his hat and dropped it. For a moment Maggie, watching, thought the puppeteer had erred. But the monk stumbled over his own hat, fell to the ground.

It was then Karaghiosi appeared. He rushed to the aid of the monk and picked him up and stood him on his feet. The two men leaned together in the middle of the screen. Their first embrace turned quickly to argument.

"She wants to be left alone," Karaghiosi said.

"She does not."

"She does so."

"She does not."

The voice of the monk was almost but not quite that of Papa B. Papa B, trying to imitate his own voice, was hesitating.

"She does so," Karaghiosi said. "Look at her."

"Look at who?" the monk said.

Karaghiosi struck the monk.

It was then Maggie intruded. She knew enough about Karaghiosi to know that he was supposed to receive the beating, not give it. "Stop, Karaghiosi," she said.

"Stop, Karaghiosi," the monk on the screen said. Then he spoke to Maggie where she sat at her desk. "Tell him you don't want to be alone," he said.

Abruptly Maggie stood up and went to the head of the stairs. She glanced back only briefly. Then she dashed down the steep stairs and closed behind her the door to the attic and raced down the next flight of stairs to her telephone.

She dialled Midnight Pizza and using a fake voice asked for Inez Catonio's home number. Ida, instead of giving the number, asked, "When are we going to see you, Maggie?"

I am at seventy hardly an old man. Yet again men are the butt of the joke in many a performance. Senex something or other. But, old or not, I guessed what Maggie had not been able to guess about herself. She could not, that second night, bear the directness of the puppets' approach. One of the puppets was asking her simply to play herself, and Maggie found the assignment impossible.

She stayed away from the attic for two days running. At midnight on the fifth day she went empty-handed up the attic stairs. Karaghiosi came onto the screen, carrying neither a club nor a pizza, but rather a camera. He carried a camera that was larger than his own head.

It was the camera that captured Maggie's attention. She began, on the dark side of the screen, to pose. She was, at first, unable to move at all, because, while watching Karaghiosi's antics with the camera, she thought of Karen Strike, and the thought of Karen fixed Maggie into literal stillness. She could not move a hand or a knee, she could not open a button or raise a hem.

Only after a long while did Maggie think of the wedding dress. The puppets on the screen were busy with each other, admiring the house, admiring each other and themselves. Maggie slipped away, unheard, she believed; she went down to her bedroom and took the wedding dress out of the closet and carried it up to the attic. She laid it across the sofa and sat down again at the desk.

Maggie, telling the story to the page as I watched, reported that on that fifth night in the attic, she, at least, or she and Karaghiosi both, began to sense the presence of a stranger.

Surely I was that stranger. Had I intruded myself into their passion? Had I been invited? Was Papa B, behind his little gang of puppets, somehow calling into Maggie's presence a presence that was mine? Who was the puppet, who the puppeteer?

Maggie remembered, in her impatience with her own delay, that Karen Strike took the pictures not for herself, but for me.

Had Papa B guessed that Maggie did her doing for my eyes, not his, he would have been mightily offended. Granted, he could not in any case see past his own puppets to the audience beyond the screen. And I am, as my ophthalmologist so evasively puts it, not gone blind but going. My glasses, as she once said, at least make me look wise. But there is seeing and there is seeing.

Maggie struck the poses that invited the puppets through the screen and into her own desperate life. She was lover and loved one both. I, the strange presence, gave a permission that poor Papa B, crouched behind his makeshift puppets, could not; my presence bared itself in the polished lens of Karaghiosi's camera eye.

The camera persuades. Maggie took off her clothes, there in the pale darkness. Her beloved Karaghiosi had not always been the outcast, the joke. It was the moving picture that destroyed the great Karaghiosi figures of the past, that turned them from teachers into clowns. Karaghiosi, in that attic, with his camera held not in front of his head but over it, recovered what had been lost. Maggie took off her clothes. She liked the undressing, the stripping down that returned her to something she had lost or forgotten or perhaps never known. She must undress in order to undress. If, to accomplish that, she must imagine the presence of a stranger, so be it. I was content to be the supreme puppet of her imagination, let Papa B connive as he might. Maggie took off her panties, her brassiere. That she might have touched herself was part of our shared pleasure, hers and mine, for she was released and so was I, by our Karaghiosi.

He spoke pizza as if it was a language. Crab meat and the rainbow colours of ripening fruit fell together on his tongue. Kiwi. Mango. He wanted mozzarella, wondered at quails' eggs. Garlic butter and a trace of goat. He remembered the taste of lark from a night in Sicily, the skin of a fish from a beach in Thailand where the sunset closed like a lover's mouth onto an opened mussel shell. He offered lichen twisted into the dried and shredded slices of a reindeer's heart, with jalapeno peppers.

Maggie listened and waited, wearing only the shades of translucent dark against her damp skin. Watching, she knew that she watched herself being watched; it was hardly the puppet's words that mattered. She wanted. And who was it, then, that approached her in the black of that fifth night? Whose body did she hold to her own? Why did she, then, for him, against him, put on the wedding dress?

Maggie Wilder studied madly the faces of clocks and watches. All day she was busy, scribbling down her inadequate notes at the kitchen table, shopping for two while she pretended to be one, dusting the dusted furniture, vacuuming the vacuumed floors. She waited for night, refusing the version of night that Dorf offered by day with his blocked windows. Only night, she insisted, could be night. On long afternoons she hid herself in the wet, crowded streets, as if I must be there too, a presence, a familiar.

She tried her key to the door. Then she realized she had stopped in front of the small house that was Josie's; she knocked.

Time had not happened for Josie and Ida. They did not so much hold conversations as recite them.

"Good to see you're still kicking," Ida said, motioning Maggie in, not for a moment losing track of the argument she was having with Josie.

"With Bludgett," Ida said. "You mark my words, birds of a feather flock together."

"I guess they do," Josie said.

Maggie sat down at the cutting table. She tried not to notice the headless torsos that crowded at her back, the chesterfield buried under cut pieces of fabric.

"With Fish, if you ask me." Josie glared brightly at Ida, at Maggie. She took a length of thread from between her lips. "Those two men in cahoots right from day one. You drive up to Deadman Spring tomorrow you'll find your nephew sitting in the pool, pretending to learn Russian from those Doukhobors. And all the while he'll be trying to collect their recipes for homemade pies for delivery to Jack Deemer."

"Hounded," Ida said.

"Once a murderer, twice a murderer." Josie asked Maggie to stand up off a pair of scissors she was sitting on.

Maggie excused herself and walked past the cup Ida was offering and went to the door.

They met each night in the attic. They were the puppets, Maggie and Dorf, not Karaghiosi. That ancient Greek shadow puppet became master. It was he who manipulated their desire. His shaping hands were mysterious gifts that fell from the dark and onto ears and nipples. Karaghiosi, that slave and fool, became master. His mouth surprised their mouths, their thighs, with urgent raids. He was the suddenness of teeth, the quickness of a tongue. In the blank dark his long fingers turned pages. Knees and fate collided, as they will, as well I know. Maggie was almost frightened, surely, and in the veil of her fright she let her own hands fall into his hair as he buried his head. She lifted him up. She let her pleased hands swarm on his empty face, finding her own desire on his kissing lips. Then and there they were two bodies, one pulse. Crying out they were a voice, Maggie taking the pain of Karaghiosi's heave.

They were exchanged for each other, and again. They were orphaned into rhapsodies of desire. He was only the breath that fell across her belly, between her thighs, into the places where the arches of her feet entered his reaching hands. "Karaghiosi," she said, calling him back. She said the name, making a small experiment into the naming of a wish. The whispered name was a reassurance to her own wet tongue, and she wondered whose hair touched her small breasts. She smelled her way to release, tasting her own desire on his lifted cock. They were a frenzy of silence. They laughed, then, after, finding shirts and socks, pyjama bottoms and the cold cups of brassieres, there in the rank dark. Finding other names.

10

On the fourteenth night the figure that came onto the screen at exactly midnight was a woman in a wedding dress.

Maggie thought at first it was herself she saw, finally more than a voice in the house that appeared and disappeared and reappeared on the screen. Then she realized the figure was not herself at all, but rather Julie Magnuson.

The figure of Julie Magnuson, wearing a wedding dress, strikes me as absurd. Consider her mob of lovers. But Papa B was having a fantasy of some sort, surely, and blatantly he pictured it there for poor Maggie to have to see.

The figure of Julie didn't speak. Perhaps Papa B didn't yet trust himself to speak in her voice. He had placed, off to one side of his screen, a cliff of cardboard and cellophane, a yellow Portuguese cliff with a green cork oak below. No doubt he intended to push poor Julie right straight off the cliff. But the story got the better of him. He had put her into a wedding dress of his own devising, a flouncy, billowy thing. He left his bride standing in the middle of the screen, unable to speak, unable to move. He could find no voice, no motion, to give her.

It was then that Maggie, whatever else she might have done, went down to the kitchen, phoned in an order.

Perhaps brides are a form of light.

Inez Catonio herself delivered the pizza. Maggie saw the box of pizza and the face of Inez Catonio and the curtain of rain behind, and her mouth went dry, her tongue curled in her mouth.

"Inez! Sorry to keep you waiting." She gestured over her right shoulder. "I was upstairs."

"Can I come in out of the weather?"

"Please do, yes."

Maggie felt a wave of terror that was at the same time a wave of relief. She had been found out. She could go to the gallows her lips sealed, no blindfold over her eyes. Weeping men would compose ballads in her honour. She would wear no drapery over her head as she fell into the emptiness beneath her feet.

"I've got to talk," Inez said.

"Coffee or beer? All I've got in the house is beer. We came make some coffee in a jiffy."

"Make it a beer." Inez was in the kitchen, she was collapsing into a chair at the kitchen table. "I've been making all deliveries to the people who ask that Papa B make the delivery."

The clock in the hallway was ticking again.

"People miss the man. He was some kind of saint, Maggie. Picking up groceries for shut-ins. Looking after kids and canaries and cats and God knows what else. Putting newspapers and mail out of sight for people who were away. Raking leaves. And yet all I want to do is kill the man."

Maggie went to the fridge and took out two bottles of beer. She reached down two dusty glasses from an open shelf. Disaster. But her hands refused to tremble. She found an opener in a drawer and lifted off the twist-off caps, then decided to wipe the glasses clean before pouring and couldn't find a towel. The kitchen seemed strange. She felt she had not been in it in a long time.

"I hope," Inez said, "you don't mind — my barging in like this."

"Not at all."

Maggie wanted to reach out and touch her.

"And Josie and Ida now. On top of everything else."

"What are those two up to?" Maggie noticed the typewriter was on and reached and turned it off. "They've opened a detective agency."

Inez was looking around the kitchen. "You need one calendar that's up to date."

"And you wonder why I don't know what day it is."

Inez laughed. "I'm coming apart, Maggie. Why did I ever stop riding herd on sagebrush and rattlesnakes?"

Maggie laughed in turn, beginning to relax. But then she thought of Papa B. There was no way to caution him. Surely he'd hear voices. And then he'd think she was on the phone — or he'd flush the toilet. He was certain to pick this time to slip down the stairs to the bathroom, the man had absolutely no normal male bathroom habits that might be mapped and charted.

"We might as well sample this damned pizza," Inez said. "Prosciutto and kiwi slices. Now where in hell did you get that one? And by the way, Ida was delighted to hear you ordering again. She says it's a good sign, you work like a slave."

Now it was Inez who went to the cupboards to find plates and napkins and a knife. Maggie sat down at the table, hardly able to lift a hand.

Inez opened the box. "Were you planning to eat this monster all by yourself?"

"No." Maggie heard her own error. She pretended to be surprised, looking into the pizza's huge green eyes. "Yes. I get three meals out of one of these. I should go buy myself a microwave." She tried to change the subject. "Tomorrow maybe. I'll drop in on Ida on the way."

"Try to get there when Fish isn't around, believe me."

Maggie was stumped into silence. Fish. Inez had said Fish's name. Maggie thinking, he has figured it out. He has guessed that Papa B is hiding here in my attic, it's perfectly logical, where else on the face of the earth would he hide, why did it take him so long to come down from the mountains and make his announcement?

"He's in the city? Fish?"

"That's putting it mildly. He's in Midnight Pizza from late afternoon to closing time. He's a fixture. He's taken to helping Ida and Elizabeth. He thinks he knows how to wait tables."

Watching. Fish was there to watch, wait. He was assuming that sooner or later Papa B wouldn't be able to stay away. Obviously, he didn't know Papa B.

Or perhaps he did. Perhaps he knew what Maggie didn't know; he knew that late one night one of Papa B's puppets would say to Papa B, let's have another pizza. Call in the order and I'll go pick it up. And Papa B would say, no, let me do it, and he'd walk out the front door and straight to Midnight Pizza and Fish would be sitting there waiting for him.

I'd be free, Maggie thought. And then she said, "Where does he sleep? I should say hello."

"On a chesterfield in Josie's living room. He's helping them pack. You'd think they were getting ready to tackle Mt Everest."

Maggie felt panic. "They're going back to Deadman Spring?"

"Not likely. They're taking a vacation. Fish says he owes them a big one. He showed up here with tickets and reservations and travel plans."

"Fish is taking a vacation? From his vacation, I take it."

"Deemer is putting him to work. Fish used to be an engineer, you know."

"He fixes leaking taps. He told me that himself."

"Not this time, he isn't. He's looking at some famous spa somewhere in Italy because Jack Deemer wants to turn Deadman Spring into the real thing. Whatever the hell that might turn out to be."

Inez raised her beer bottle and took a long swallow. "My God it feels good to be here." She drank again. "I'm a wreck, Maggie. A total fucking wreck. I've been through hell and back without drawing a normal breath. One thing I don't need is men, and another thing I don't need is men. So I called in the police to find one that is missing." She tasted a slice of pizza. "I called in the police. Now they're watching all my pizza places. I hired a detective. I don't dare tell him anything because I think he's working for someone else. What should I do?"

"Buy a ranch," Maggie said.

They were talking then, and eating pizza.

"We laugh, Maggie. But I'm serious, I'm going to kill that guy Papa B when I find him. There's nothing else I can do. Nothing."

"I wish I could believe you."

"I have no choice. Really. It's the only way I'll ever get back the sanity I had before that lunk came begging at my door. I'm telling you. I'm going to fire my detective. I'm going to pay a thug I know. It'll cost me two free pizzas and a bottle of wine." Inez put down the slice of pizza she wasn't eating. "And where's your toilet? I'm about ready to wet my pants every twenty-eight minutes."

Maggie wanted to raise her hands in the air and shout, it's in the attic, the john. And take that knife with you. There's an axe in the basement, I'll get you that. "Straight up the stairs. End of the hall. If you're running, watch out for the rug. It slides."

Inez went upstairs. Maggie sat at the kitchen table, unable to swallow the food in her mouth. The clock in the hallway marked time with tremors that came from under water. Minutes went by. Hours. Days. Inez must be stuck, she can't get the bathroom door open. Why did she lock it, who was she expecting to burst in on her? Or maybe this is all a bluff, her clever little scheme to get into the house and have a look around, she's up in the attic right now, dumbfounded and murderous.

Maggie had time to study her four calendars. Ida and Josie were heading off to some Italian spa with Fish. Maybe they'd stay forever. She'd borrow the key to Josie's house, offer to water the Boston fern, use the house as a place to hide Papa B. She'd set him up on his own, let him make one actual decision in his long life.

The windows shook in their casings. Somewhere above her head, a cascade of water entered the failing sewer system. Old houses had their virtues.

Inez was in the kitchen doorway. "I guess I ought to be on my way. I told Fish I'd meet him. He's got some cockeyed theory that Papa B is hiding in Italy. Some spa that De Medeiros used to be famous in, when he was alive and kicking."

"You said he's going to look at spas for Deemer."

"That's what Deemer thinks. Poor old Deemer. Fish put the bee in his bonnet. Deemer put up the cash because he thinks he'd like to live forever." Inez turned away, then called over her shoulder, "He can have it."

And then Fish too was gone. Maggie found out from Ida that he had gone back to Deadman Spring to make architectural drawings, to measure water flow, and to chart the weather. Jack Deemer wanted to build for comfort as well as for immortality.

She could not invite Papa B to her bedroom. They were lovers in the attic only, taking care not to meet on the second floor of the house. March was a blur of tulips and darkness. April fell out of the sky. Maggie, under a variety of umbrellas, went into the streets to buy more paints, more paper, more cellophane. Papa B, there in his attic, made a sun and a moon. He set Maggie to looking in catalogues and books and magazines for a hundred objects, the profile of a Mercedes, the outline of a particular kind of gun.

His version of Jack Deemer had a calendar for a head, a pair of spectacles where one might have expected his private parts. His arms were six, and certainly not human, his fingertips each concealed in a thimble. His legs, attached to the outline of an old-fashioned wooden cradle, were rows of dominoes. His eyes were Chinese copper coins, each with a square hole in its centre. And out of this dog's breakfast, Papa B contrived to make a story as monstrous as the man.

I have not done things by halves in my life, granted. Fish was a competitor for Julie Magnuson's hand. Papa B got that much straight. But, in the little show he put on for Maggie, hoping by that perversity to awaken her to other perverse longings, he had me bury Fish alive.

Fish at the time was a mining engineer, with a dream of the easy dollar. The Japanese were looking for thermal coal. Fish remembered the abandoned mines and towns of his youth. He was stupid enough to walk down into a mine shaft by himself — and then have the entrance collapse behind him.

Perhaps he shouted loud and direct, into the deserted shaft, to see if it is true that shouting can bring down coal and rock. That would be the most likely story, to anyone knowing Fish. But Papa B, in his ignorance, put on a great show that made me look the villain. He managed to invent in his pitiful charade, right there at the mine's entrance, the explosion of a few sticks of dynamite. The trick had its desired effect. Maggie was frightened half to death; she rushed into the trap once more.

When Fish, on someone's anonymous tip, was discovered alive but terribly hungry, he was reported to have said — though he later denied it — that he would rather eat breakfast than get married.

Julie Magnuson took him at his word.

I had worn a new suit to what was to have been the wedding of Fish and Julie. I was, at the church door, handed a corsage.

Papa B, in his own perverse lust, had Jack Deemer rush directly from the explosion into the hotel where the bride was to change clothes. They were at once visible and invisible, man and wife, behind the cellophane windows, some of those windows a lavender shade, some violently purple, some almost a blood red.

When the dress fell onto the small hooked rug on the bare wooden floor in that stark room, we fell upon the dress, Julie and I. We were a part of the scheme and design and tapestry that graced the dress. Julie was naked, and I too took off my clothes. We fell into flowers and trees. Poor Fish, come tardy and lame to the day, was no doubt somewhere having his rasher of bacon, his favourite omelette with home fries on the side and loud gobs of ketchup on the fries and on the omelette too. Julie and I were as careful as gentians with each other, as rough as mountain junipers. The infinite threads caressed us. The small beads were not rough at all but rather served as goads to our infinite and various motion. In the tumult of the dress we were the story that Josie Pavich had only guessed; we were the lovers in animal form that she had so carefully pictured, the man with the body of a fish, the horse-headed man, the woman with octopus arms. Upstairs in that shabby hotel room, in that hotel that now, like the town before it, must have become ghost, we let ourselves sweat and whisper. Our mouths took measure. We fell out of words, into the wonder of our inexhaustible bodies. Our fingers spread the difference, or closed it small. We cried out, shouted, and with our gasping mouths began again. And always the dress was our bed and our inspiration.

11

I've been thinking," Bludgett said.

"That seems unlikely." Maggie, quickly, got into the car. She'd been waiting on the porch, to keep Bludgett from ringing the doorbell.

"I think Inez is holding him prisoner." Bludgett was pleased with himself, persuaded that his sleepless nights were producing results. "I've got it figured out. There's only one place where Papa B can possibly be hiding."

"And where would that be, Thomas?"

They were driving away from Maggie's house, going out to dinner. Or at least Bludgett, in his aggressive and uncertain way, had said that was the intention.

"Inez has him locked up in that mansion of hers. I'll bet you my bottom dollar."

"Okay, I'll bet you."

"What do you want to bet?"

"First off, how are we going to prove anything?"

"We're going to Inez's house to take a look."

"I'll bet you two cents." Maggie reached to the door handle. "Let me out here. That would be housebreaking, Thomas. Maybe you haven't heard. That wouldn't look good on a lawyer's record. Even if you claim that you are no longer a lawyer. Even if you lawyers do love your criminals."

"I still have a key. She's at work at this hour."

"No, Thomas. . . . We can't do it. You cannot do it."

Maggie thought of Papa B breaking into her own house, pushing open the basement door in the middle of a rainy night. She couldn't do the same now, she couldn't, even if Bludgett had a key. She simply wouldn't do it. She had wondered long about the house, about how they lived together, Papa B and Inez. But she would not risk that threshold.

"You're playing detective, Thomas."

"Not at all. Your Papa B — he seems to have all hell on his case."

Maggie knew she must talk to Bludgett, take him into her confidence. She had to trust him, though every impulse told her not to. If she went along with Bludgett now, she'd find an opportunity to speak.

Bludgett, after hesitating at an intersection, made a left turn. He swung up toward the university. Then, before Maggie could gather her wits about her, he was pointing through the near darkness at a turret. A high turret rose on a corner of the nearest house. The house itself was partially concealed by bushes and trees. The turret, a shadow against the illumined night sky, was patched with dark squares that must be windows.

"We can't," Maggie said, hating the adrenaline that was telling her, do it or run.

Bludgett was parking the car.

"I take it it didn't work?" Maggie was talking over the voice that told her, jump out of the car, run and hide.

"What didn't work? We're doing fine."

"Your being lovers. You and Inez."

"We weren't doing too badly. Then Papa B came along."

"And then?"

"In a way, I was grateful." Bludgett was locking the car. "In some awful way . . . I was failing. Just as she told you. But the trouble was — well, I was doing it on purpose, Maggie. I was doing it to please Inez."

He started across the street.

Maggie hesitated to follow. "And we're doing this too — walking up to her front door, entering her house — just to please her?"

"Were you listening? I said that we're doing this for Papa B."

"You didn't quite answer my question."

"I was trying not to hear it."

They were walking arm in arm up the long walkway, through a miniature forest of bushes and trees. Bludgett took a key from a pocket of his tweed jacket.

"No alarms?" Maggie said.

"Inez is more afraid of the cops than she is of burglars. Alarms would only attract attention."

"That's why she called in the cops to find her missing man."

"My hunch is she did that to make herself look innocent. Inez knows how to walk down both sides of the street at once. And she loves to watch herself doing it."

They stepped inside the tall front door and Bludgett pushed it shut. He found a light switch.

"Good God, Thomas. You aren't going to turn on the lights."

"The windows in this house are mostly fake." Bludgett pointed at two balconies, one on either side of a huge fireplace. "One of those is fake. One of those is real. I forget which is which."

Maggie, silently, followed after Bludgett. He moved with new confidence up a long marble stairway, then to another.

The tower they'd seen from outside was, it turned out, a bathroom. The windows on the outside of the tower were fake, there were no windows inside.

"I thought you'd been here before," Maggie said, responding to Bludgett's surprise.

"I was. And when I was here — this room was a little courtroom." He returned to his hesitant way, laughing. "She liked to try me. In court." He pointed to the stepped platform covered in black marble that looked like a small stage.

"It turned her on?"

"You're a genius."

"And you?"

He shrugged. "She'd sentence me — to do whatever she wanted me to do. Then I'd have to be my own lawyer."

"How could you lose?"

The bathroom was huge, at once stark and lavish, a composition in black, with only enough gold to make the black blacker. The sunken tub at the centre of the room was of polished black marble, with the black of the tub surrounded by black marble floors. The angled ceiling, the high walls, the toilet, the twin basins were of black marble. The fixtures over the basins were of gold. The dimly shining lamps on the black marble walls were set in translucent marble flecked with gold.

"Fucking gross," Bludgett said.

"Look," Maggie pointed. "Black toilet paper. Now we're getting real."

Bludgett pressed a button and waited as if Papa B would have to appear through an invisible door. Water fell in small cascades down the stepped black marble platform. The huge tub began to fill.

"You've seen this before?"

"I've never been to Deadman Spring. You have."

Maggie said nothing.

"This is the cave, isn't it? The place where the mineral water falls out of the rock."

"We didn't go into the cave. Fish wouldn't take us in."

Bludgett was taking off his shoes and socks. He was taking off his clothes. "She said to me one day, 'You only know the rules, Thomas, and how to bend them. I need a lover who could aim a gun at his own soul.

And pull the trigger.' That was the night of the day she met Papa B."

"I take it the renovations began soon after."

Bludgett laughed. "Let's see if Papa B finds us here. Let's see if we can lure him into view."

Maggie, undressing, saw herself variously in the soft, hard shine of marble. Mist lifted above the water. She was not undressing at all for Bludgett.

She was, to her surprise and embarrassment and satisfaction, undressing for Inez. She removed her clothes and dropped them onto the marble floor. Bludgett, below her in the tub, moved deliberately and without will in his gentle wish to surrender to the woman from whom he had escaped. Or been sent away. He was obedient and appalling. He knelt in the water, the soles of his feet comically, ridiculously, beautifully vulnerable, his buttocks raised, as he bent to the slowly rising water. He bent to taste and inhale. Maggie stepped down and knelt beside him. The oiled and salted water tasted of thyme, of orange. It tasted of sage and oregano. A desert, Bludgett suggested, dissolved into sea. Seaweed, Maggie suggested, low tide and seaweed. They were together in the water, Maggie and Bludgett, tasting the herbal bath, the mineral edge. They raised up and inhaled. Limestone. Iron. Clay. The dryness of cork. Lemon peel, twisted, touched against the juniper of gin.

"Leave it to the pizza queen," Bludgett said. "Extra large. Loaded."

They wanted to be found out. They wanted to be caught, by Papa B, by Inez. Maggie, watching the reflections in the marble surfaces around her, knew that Papa B was caught in her attic, trying to tell himself a story that would let him back into the world. And yet she wanted him somehow to appear in the doorway that vanished into the seamless marble of the high walls. She wanted him to come stooping through the wall, led by Inez.

She thought of Henry Ketch, leading her into the small forests of candles in Byzantine churches. Icons. Puppets. She had wanted to make love there too, in the holy forests of Henry's dream, and Henry had been embarrassed.

Papa B. With his pizza queen. Dipping his face into the water to kiss with his whole mouth the lifted weight of her arrival home. His tongue as hot as the water. Maggie would let herself be Inez. She lay her head back into the water, letting her body float against his tongue. His hands flowed to her floating buttocks and she was deliciously drowning. His tongue rode the delicate, lapped surface like a mysterious fish. She wanted to whisper, William. Dorf. Papa B. But the water was there, waiting, to flood her opened mouth.

Maggie asked Bludgett to make love to her. He said he couldn't. One hardly need be surprised.

"You might at least try. You might pretend."

Bludgett, seated, naked, splashed softly in the water. "Force me to."

"You're out of your mind, Thomas."

"Charge me with breaking and entering." He let himself laugh into raised handfuls of water. "Hold my head under the water. See how long I can hold my breath."

"Thomas, you're a lunatic. That woman wrecked you."

"Her husband killed himself," Thomas said. "I'm not as wrecked as he was."

"She told me they were divorced."

"They were divorced. Then, after she threw him out —" Abruptly, Bludgett stood up in the tub. He found on a ledge beside the cascading water a large black towel. He looked down at Maggie, floating on her back while gently she kicked the soles of her lifted feet against the tumble of water. He turned away, stepped up out of the tub.

"We could be nasty," he said. "We could make it look as if Papa B had dropped by."

"That would be cruel, not nasty."

"I guess you won the bet. Okay. Now where do we look?"

"Maybe we should stop looking."

"I have to get him out of the picture. Somehow. Don't I?"

I am going to abandon him. Maggie wrote that in her notes when she was safe in her kitchen again. She was going to abandon Papa B, she would leave him to starve, there in the attic. He could patch together his puppets, play out their story until they told him what to do. And he could train them to go out and buy bread and milk and coffee. Because she would be gone.

She went to pay a visit to Josie's small house. She watched for a gap between showers, then walked through the Vancouver streets on carpets of fallen petals. She found the house. She knocked at the front door.

A man answered the door. "Surprise," he said.

Fish stood tall and grey-bearded in the doorway, wearing his toque. And a very old suit. And a new shirt still showing its fold creases.

"Come in," he said. "Come in, come in."

Maggie somehow wanted to produce from behind her back a boxed pizza. Plain. Loaded. The whole shebang. Here it is, it's all yours, enjoy. And oh yes, I have some news.

"Who is it, Fish?" Ida was somewhere in the basement, calling.

"That famous hermit we were talking about."

"Maggie!" Josie appeared from the kitchen.

Ida came up the basement stairs with a battered brown suitcase in one hand, a damp dishcloth in the other. "Maggie. I just about dropped by to see if we could borrow a suitcase."

And then Josie and Ida together were explaining: they were leaving for the airport. They'd have a light lunch and leave, Josie was making a lunch right that minute, hurry, they said, stay for lunch, they said. Fish, they said, was taking them to Rome. He had work to do, they'd be on their own, the two women. And they weren't going to waste their time on the old stuff, sites and relics, no, they were heading straight for one of the spas that Fish was looking at.

"My arthritis is killing me today," Ida said.

"That kind of arthritis comes in a jug, Ida. Maggie, you should have seen Ida last night."

The two old women were delighted, scared, excited, dependent on Fish and giving him orders. Maggie, thinking, I gave this up to live alone, if living with Papa B in one's attic can be called living alone. I gave it up after dinner one night, the four of us, Henry and me, Geoff and David, at the dinner table, talking and not talking, Henry with the letter beside his plate on the dinner table, the Guggenheim confirmed in the assurance of print, he was going to Greece for a year; the two boys then, seeing the gap in the fence, the door left slightly ajar, declaring their excuses, Mom, we'll take care of ourselves. And maybe I wanted that too, I wanted Henry to make his lofty pronouncements that disguised his delight at getting away. I sat there that night at the table, my three men present and already gone. I sat over my glass of a Greek wine that Henry claimed to have discovered, though I'd told him about it first. I sat there, watching the candles consume themselves over the gravy boat and the last golden ring of pineapple and the white linen tablecloth that I'd hauled back from Athens in a shopping bag. I sat there that night, talking and not talking, daring at last to think if not to say a few words about what it felt like to want the nest to break from the swaying tree and crash to the ground.

"I'm planning a trip myself," Maggie said.

"Just don't go to Deadman Spring." Josie was wiping out the inside of the old suitcase that Ida had found in the basement. "Not while Fish is away. That awful Karen Strike is going to run the place."

Maggie addressed her reply to the headless dress forms, there in the living room, avoiding Josie and Ida and Fish. "I'm going to fly to Greece. Just as soon as I get some loose ends tidied up."

"You're going to see Henry," Ida said. "He hit the nail right on the head, didn't he?"

"Darn." Josie put down her dust cloth on her cutting table, then searched her sleeves for her handkerchief. "We were going to get you to check this place every couple of days. Just drop by. Maybe water the plants."

"Shake hands with the doorknob," Ida added. "Mow the grass. Spray our apple tree. Maybe dig up that back garden. You're lucky you'll be gone."

"At least I'll water your plants." Maggie, the resolve announced, heard herself retreating. "I plan to arrive in Greece just when the swimming gets good. I'll be here till you get back, I promise."

"It's not the house." Josie was picking dead fronds off the Boston fern. "Would you believe it, Ida thinks the minute we're gone, Papa B will show up at our door."

"Let him stay here till we get back. Just don't tell Inez where he's hiding."

And then Maggie was making excuses for her having to rush off, asking them to send postcards, saying hello to Fish. She promised to check the house every day, she'd walk over, she said, the exercise would do her good.

Ida was folding sweaters into the suitcase. "Stay for some of Josie's lentil soup."

"I made enough food for an army," Josie said.

Maggie protested, standing in the open doorway, no, she had to hurry.

"We're about two hours ahead of schedule." Fish was trying to stay out of Ida's way and getting in the way of Josie and lunch. "These women have only been cleaning, ironing, laundering, and packing for two weeks. Please slow them down."

"We'll bring you some lunch." Josie was pushing a cut-glass dish of dill pickles and corn relish into Fish's hands. "It's hardly out of our way at all." And Fish was nodding over his shoulder toward Maggie, yes, please, agree to anything. Ida held up another sweater, started to fold it. "Waste not want not, that's what Josie always says."

And then Maggie couldn't resist. She said, okay, she'd be at home, they could drop by, they could drop off the food. They could even, she added, have a beer before they caught their flight, if they had time.

She put on her wedding dress. She was planning an exit.

Maggie sat at her kitchen table. Perhaps, she typed, every autobiography is a decoy. Even that of a wedding dress.

Obiter. She imagined Bludgett looking over her shoulder. *Obiter dicta,* Maggie Wilder. Not to the point. There is only one life available, at best, to each of us. Wear it for real. That same Thomas Bludgett who couldn't wake up because he didn't know how to fall asleep.

She tried to imagine the two old women discovering Rome, forgetting about their spa. They will like their daily walks, she typed, their evening visits to a trattoria for a perfect Italian meal, with cappuccino after, and grappa after cappuccino. They will like the deep sleep that follows, in the purring, hot dark of the Roman night.

She stopped. No. She was remembering her own visit to Italy. With Henry. They were on their way to Athens, they stopped in Rome, at her insistence, Henry impatient. Henry, briefly in the Vatican Museum, speculating on the absence of the reds and golds that made Byzantine icons resist the daily tick of the clock. And all the while she was lost in the wild beauty of broken Roman bricks and the sudden speech of flowers.

Obiter, Maggie.

She was thinking of Rome and its ancientness and the builders who did not ever see the ruins that were her joy, when the doorbell rang. She had flung open the door before she remembered she had on her wedding dress.

"Coffee," Ida said. "We have time for a quick cup of coffee. No booze."

Josie dropped the food she was carrying. She dropped the platter of sliced ham that was not yet cold, the dill pickles, the corn relish, the plate of johnnycake, the loaf and a half of homemade white bread, the celery slices stuffed with cheese, the pie platter and its four wedges of blackberry pie.

"Butterfingers," Ida said.

They were, the three of them, trying to pick up the scattered food.

"Don't get that pie on the dress," Josie said.

"Leave it." Maggie backed away from the mess on the floor. "Just leave it. Come in. I'll clean up later."

They were into the hallway, Josie and Ida.

"Where's Fish?"

"He's in the car." Ida sampled some of the pie, then stood up, licking her fingers. "He drank his lunch. He's resting. We all drank our lunch."

Josie was touching Maggie's dress. She touched the hem of the dress. Then she straightened, letting her fingers caress the needlework, the almost invisible beadwork. Perhaps at that very moment, she became confused.

"You look great," she said. To Maggie.

"Thank you."

"Fish will love it."

"Just let him catch his forty winks."

Josie was confused, looking at the dress she had so long ago spent days and weeks preparing, and then preparing again. "You can't do that to him, Julie."

Or perhaps she was not confused at all. Josie's idea of drinking was having a sip of Ida's wine.

She was arguing with Julie Magnuson. She was fitting her, helping her dress for the wedding. Josie reached to the embroidered silk buttons, closed one that was open.

"Quick," Maggie said. "How much time have we got?"

It was Maggie who panicked. "Quick," she said again. "We have time. Just barely. Come up to the attic. Quick."

12

The attic was as dark as the mines that Josie Pavich visited with her father when she was a child. Maggie, wedged between the two old women, reached in the dark to find Ida's hand. In her reaching, Maggie stepped backwards herself, and it was Ida who found her, there in the dark, with both hands, and steadied her. The three women, noisy, boisterous, scared and pretending to be scared, crowded up the narrow stairway.

A distant light came on. A light came on far back in the attic. It was not Maggie's house, this time, on the screen. It was a hotel flying the green and red Portuguese flag. It was a grand hotel on a sandy beach on the Algarve coast of Portugal.

"Look," Josie said, leading the way. Ida stepped up on the attic floor beside Maggie. They stopped at the top of the stairs, fascinated by the lit screen and its line of beach and its luxury hotel.

A figure came out of the hotel's entrance — and indeed that hotel was a far cry from the two-story wooden crate in which Julie and I had our fierce encounter. The small figure was that of a dwarf. He was a handsome man with long yellow hair and wide blue eyes. He was wearing a blouse that might have been made from the petals of violets.

Now it was Ida who said, "Look." She poked at the other women. "That's the drowned man. He's right there, alive as the smile on your face."

Josie's voice went weak with excitement. "Now isn't he a dilly."

The figure of De Medeiros spoke. "I am at your service," he called.

The pompous fraud. Josie Pavich did not recognize that it was not she whom he addressed. I wish I had been there. Why did not the concealed manipulator bring onto his screen the puppet that was myself? But no such luck. And no such courage either, on his part. He knew I would have raised my fist against the very puppet master himself.

Maggie and Josie and Ida stayed at the top of the stairs. Their eyes were adjusting to the muted light.

It was then that Maggie saw what was happening. The attic itself had become part of Papa B's puppet show. He had gone through the frame. The attic and the story he purported to tell had become one and the same for their precious Papa B.

Maggie's borrowed attic was littered with botanical specimens, with fronds and leaves and petals and blossoms, with unrecognizable shapes, all of them smelling faintly of faraway rain forests. And all of them flattened and dried. Poor Papa B, slick and clean out of his mind, in making and elaborating his gaudy little show, had unpacked most of George's crates and bales and garbage bags. The attic had become a grotesque mausoleum, a funeral home for a fool's dead dream.

"Good health to you, sir." Josie said. She was ready to sign up right there.

Papa B, in his days and nights of working with his puppets, had lost every trace of his own voice. The voice he represented was that of Dr Manuel De Medeiros. I can only assume he managed the impersonation well, since Billy Dorfendorf's own voice, when he worked in my employ, was edgy, nervous, always looking for an escape. De Medeiros spoke with a measured confidence. He assumed he had a curative voice.

"I have the keys to the car," he said.

I would have given a million dollars to be a figure on that screen. I would have explained, shouted, exposing Dr Manuel De Medeiros for the brazen seducer that he was. Maggie's desk had vanished; or rather, it had disappeared into some version of a banyan tree. Maggie and Josie and Ida, on top of everything else, were peering through a collection of trunks and branches and leaves.

And now a second figure came out of the grand hotel. It was Julie Magnuson. But this time she did not have on her wedding dress. She did not have on a stitch of anything. She was naked as a blue jay, except for a bouquet of roses raised in her right hand. De Medeiros reached up toward the bouquet.

Josie saw what was happening. She shouted a warning to her little hero.

Julie Magnuson smashed De Medeiros over the head with the bouquet. She bammed him.

"Hit him again," Ida shouted.

But Josie was outraged. She started through that little forest of flattened leaves toward the screen.

A black Mercedes appeared beside the hotel. The man behind the array of puppets, after all, had only so many hands and fingers, and, given those limitations, he chose not to represent his own role in the scheme. Or perhaps he truly expected us to believe that he was, while all this transpired, sound asleep in bed.

Now it was Ida, rushing to Papa B's aid, who plunged into his tropical thicket, his little bower that was no doubt intended to seduce Maggie Wilder back into his power and into some further aberration. The man's imagination was vile and despicable.

Julie Magnuson and De Medeiros started at once and together toward the Mercedes.

Ida would stop them if she had to break both legs and an arm to boot.

"Hey!"

Only Maggie heard the new voice.

"Hey!" the voice called, from the bottom of the stairwell. "Anybody home?"

Maggie, softly, called, "Wait!"

"What's the hold-up? We're going to miss the flight."

"We'll be right down."

Papa B was saved by Fish. He had become his own Karaghiosi, and he was about to be pummelled by one or the other or both of those two old women. He was about to be hammered.

The voice of Fish filled the stairwell. He was on the steps. He was calling. "Ida? Is that you?"

Fish had something of a liking for Ida.

Maggie pushed half a palm tree into Fish's face.

William William Dorfendorf claimed later that he awoke late that morning, there on the Algarve beach, only to find Julie Magnuson gone from his suite of rooms, his rented Mercedes gone from the courtyard of the hotel. Papa B skipped all this. His own irresponsibilities were not to be made public.

On the screen the Mercedes simply made its exit, stage left, into the very forest of the attic. In Papa B's lurid imagination it no doubt turned north and away from the coastline, found a high cliff, fell to the long wail not of two voices but rather of one, then hung, its doors open, like a child's lost kite, like a shot bird, in the branches of a huge cork tree far below.

Josie and Maggie did not want to leave the enchanted forest. Maggie, pushing her palm fronds or her coconuts or whatever, stumbled down the steps to block Fish from seeing up into the attic. He was in a small frenzy of his own. He shouted again something about missing the flight. The worm had turned.

Fish was ready to do battle with Maggie, to get his message through to Josie and Ida. They were all shouting toward and past each other, Fish and Ida and Josie and Maggie. They shouted and jostled their way down the stairs and through the pickle juice on the floor and out the front door. They were on the porch, they were going down the steps, the three women herding Fish toward his car. They shouted back across the narrow lawn, Ida and Josie, to Maggie, standing on the steps.

"We'll see you in ten days," Josie shouted. She was in the back seat of the car. Ida was in front with Fish.

"Tell him," Ida shouted. "Tell you-know-who that we'll see the ending when we get back."

As if an ending is possible, when life is at stake.

Sometimes I wonder . . . if Fish had not been rescued from that coal mine . . . if he had been left to die the slow, damp, dark death that he so richly deserved instead of being allowed to snoop his way around the globe . . . or to limp his way. He let himself walk with a limp, but only when I was present to see it. It was one of his ways of getting revenge.

Maggie Wilder had hardly taken the trouble to visit Ida and Josie, ever, and yet their presence in the city had sustained her. And to her credit she did take the trouble to look after Josie's house. Once each day she went for a walk through the violence of cloud and sun, sometimes early in the morning, sometimes in late afternoon. She began to wonder if she might move into Josie's house, then make her daily trek from there to feed her lunatic in his high forest. That way she would not have to face the nights when she sensed his presence like a man become werewolf, up there in her dark.

Papa B no longer bothered to pick up the clean laundry she placed outside the attic door. One morning, returning from her walk to Josie's house, Maggie stopped to buy a bottle of something that would freshen the air in her bathroom and all through the house. It was beginning to smell more like a lair than a home.

Papa B called down from the attic as she, catching her breath, approached the bathroom. "The phone's been ringing off the wall for the past half-hour."

"Probably Henry," she called back. "He must be wondering when I expect to show up."

She said that to scare Papa B, and it worked. His head appeared at the top of the attic stairway.

She hadn't seen him in a few days. He appeared in a tangle of vines and husks and leaves. His face was a mass of hair that opened to let out words. Even at that distance, he smelled of his own sweat and urine.

"Something ferocious."

For a moment Maggie thought he was describing himself.

"That damned phone," Papa B said. And then he said, almost begging, "You got time for a cup of coffee?"

Maggie relented. She had been avoiding him for days, setting his food and supplies on the lowest step of the attic stairs. "Okay, okay. Hang on a minute."

She went into the bathroom first. She hadn't been able to scrub away the smell; now she would try spraying. Poison, she thought. I'll poison the shit smell out of this house.

And then he was right, the phone was ringing, ferociously.

She took her own good time. She scrubbed her hands under a tap, found a clean towel. She made her way slowly down the stairs toward the kitchen. George, putting the phone where it was, had guaranteed for himself the interruptions that would take him away from his work — all the way to Borneo.

Maggie picked up the phone. "Hello."

And then she heard Ida's voice saying, "Maggie?"

"Ida!"

"Maggie, is that you?"

"Yes."

"This is Ida."

"I recognized your voice, Ida."

"I'm in Rome. We're in Rome."

"I know that, Ida. At least that's what I've been assuming. Is everything okay?"

"We're at the Fenix Hotel. That's spelled with an F."

"What's the matter, Ida? Are you okay?"

"We've found him."

"Found who?"

For a moment Maggie believed they'd found Papa B, he wasn't that monster who had stuck his head into the attic stairwell, that beast-man calling down from the darkness. The real Papa B had escaped from her as he escaped from everyone else, he was there in Italy, in Rome. Ida and Josie had spotted him in the katacombs.

"That Manny fellow," Ida said. "That dwarf. The puppet man that is there in your attic."

She shouldn't have let them see the puppet show, Maggie realized. She said nothing.

"That guy with the yellow hair. He *does* have yellow hair. Just like the puppet. And blue eyes that would knock your wig off."

"Maggie? Are you there?"

"I'm here."

"We've been calling you for two hours. We decided we should call you. You should tell Papa B."

"Tell him what, Ida?'

"Maggie? Are you okay?"

"Are you three drinking?"

"Fish isn't with us. He went to Tivoli. He's arranging for us to go to a spa for treatments."

Josie came onto the phone. "We have been drinking. There's a perfect bar in our room. One of those little fridges, chuck full of little bottles. We like it."

"You're drunk. You're seeing things."

"Not when we saw him. We were stone-cold sober."

"That happens, Josie. When you travel, you see people who look —" Good grief, she was thrilled; her heart was pounding. "He's *dead,* Josie."

Now it was Ida who had the receiver again. "We talked to him. We were in the Piazza del Rotonda. We were having *gelato*."

"*Gelati,*" Josie called in the background.

"Dr De Medeiros? You spoke to him?"

Maggie wanted it to be true and wouldn't let herself believe. Or perhaps, she admitted to herself, she didn't want it to be true. She wanted to stay where she was, forever, with Papa B upstairs as her prisoner, a slave shackled to his crew of puppets.

They were trading the receiver back and forth, the two women, trying both to speak at once. Now it was Josie Maggie heard. "We sort of spoke to him. We heard him speak."

"He was watching us," Ida put in. "We think he was watching us."

"But you've never heard his voice." Maggie was still talking to Josie.

"We heard his voice in your attic," Ida said.

Maggie's indignation filled her own voice. "That Papa B of yours is a lunatic. The man is a failed wreck of a human being, he doesn't have a mind of his own or a tongue of his own. And now he's done this."

"Yes," Josie said. "It's wonderful."

It was that simple conviction that struck Maggie into decision. "I'll change my ticket. I'll stop in Rome. I'll get the next flight I can get. I'll come straight to your hotel. If you go to the spa, leave a message."

It was late afternoon when Maggie found herself walking in Chinatown, letting herself disappear into the jostle of shoppers who stopped, looked, hurried again. Whole barbecued chickens and large, flat, dried ducks available there under Bludgett's nose, while at a public phone he ordered in pizza.

Gai choi. Winter melon. Okra. Fish on beds of ice, fish alive in tanks. Bananas and grapes and oranges. Fresh noodles and barbecued pork buns. She resisted the impulse to feed the man before she asked him the question she carried like a block of melting ice.

She went up the two flights of stairs to Bludgett's apartment. When there was no answer she knocked again. When there was still no answer she knocked a third time.

Bludgett opened the door.

"Where were you, for God's sake?"

Bludgett signalled her into the room.

"I think maybe I dozed off."

"I'll never tell. I promise."

"Ah," he said. "Now I remember. In *Trading Places*. I think it's the last story in the book. It opens, 'I'll never tell. I promise.'"

He liked doing that to her.

Maggie reached down a teapot. She started to fill a kettle with water. "Are you awake enough for some tea?"

"I'll make it." He lifted down a basket that had in it ten Chinese teacups. "I assume you didn't come here just to find out if I sleep on the sly. You want to know what Inez had to say about our visit."

"You told her!"

"Not on your life."

"She guessed."

Again, Bludgett shook his head. "Would you believe it? She thinks Papa B was there. In her house. And we didn't even plan it that way."

"Like hell we didn't."

"Now she suspects everyone. Even you."

Maggie had her chance. She was puzzling over the label on a box of Chinese tea. "I'm going away — for a while."

"That will clear you, won't it? You'll come up smelling like roses."

"I'm going away. I mean it. Away away."

"Not to Deadman Spring again."

"No."

"To be honest — I'll miss you."

"You never see me." She lifted a stack of books off a chair and sat down. "I'm going to Greece. I'm stopping in Rome on the way — to see Ida and Josie."

"You're admitting you're beat. Henry will be delighted."

"Nothing satisfies Henry."

"And why are you stopping in Rome? To take spa treatments with Josie and Ida? Aren't you in enough hot water?"

"Funny."

"That's not how Inez describes me."

"I realized while I was climbing the stairs to your apartment that I'm here to ask a favour of you."

"Shoot."

"I want you to stay in my house while I'm gone."

Bludgett was measuring tea leaves into a bowl with a clam shell. "How do you like my new tea bowl?"

"It's a beauty."

"Ting Chou ware. Cost me a small fortune."

"How long does it take you now, to make your cup of tea?"

"A good part of the morning."

"Hang in. You'll make the process last all day."

"You got it."

"Thomas. I'm serious. I'm desperately serious."

"How long will you be gone?"

"Until I get back."

"It would give Inez's detective a change of pace. He's getting careless."

"Then you'll do it?"

Bludgett placed a stone salt dish and a bamboo spoon on his small table. "You don't have a cat. You don't have any plants. You don't have anything that a self-respecting thief would try to steal. Why, for instance, don't you buy yourself something better than a top-of-the-fridge radio? And what have you got against TV sets that work?"

"I have a living goddamned theatre in my house."

"I've never noticed it. Most of the time you're staring at a typewriter as if you might be catatonic."

"The theatre is in the attic."

Bludgett was pouring hot water. "Bats?"

"Bats all right. Batty. Your batty friend Willy Willy Batty Dorfendorf."

Bludgett, carefully, put the tea kettle back onto the stove. Teetering, he reached, took off one slipper, scratched the sole of his foot, put the slipper back on. "Tell me I'm sound asleep, Maggie. Tell me I'm simply having a nightmare."

"I had to help him."

"You'll get yourself killed for kindness."

"Do me a favour. Sometimes he can even be lovable."

"There are people around who want lovingly to tear out his tongue."

"He couldn't get anything straight if his life depended on it. Most of the time he's a mushroom."

"I tried helping him. I thought he could be helped."

"All you have to do is feed him. And water him."

"Like a pet."

"Thomas, get on with your tea business."

"I'm trying." He picked up a ladle. "This is made of pear wood. How do you like the colour?"

"You might end up tearing out his tongue yourself. And you might have to help him with his laundry. But I doubt it. . . . Just stay with him for a while. You'll have to buy his groceries. He hasn't got a red cent to his name. He likes making puppets. He's never made one that looks like you."

"Sounds like fun. How could I resist helping a friend."

"Good," Maggie said. "Then here's a key to the house. Please don't show up until I'm gone. If I so much as peek into the attic, I won't be able to leave."

"Have a ball."

"Oh." Maggie stopped. "Just one last thing. If Dr De Medeiros ever did happen to show up alive, where would that leave Papa B?"

"I don't know about Papa B. But it would leave Jack Deemer with two men to hunt to death."

13

At the Leonardo da Vinci Airport Maggie decided to take a bus rather than a taxi into the city. A taxi, she found on inquiring, would cost her a small fortune. She had two bags and a briefcase to carry, for though she'd left behind her typewriter, she'd decided at the last minute to take along her notes and files. And her wedding dress.

Palm trees and sunshine. She left her bags with the driver's assistant; ENTRATA, the sign said; she boarded the bus and pushed her way beyond the door. She let herself sway with the crowd on the bus, with the bus itself. Stooping, she caught a glimpse of groups of apartment houses on the far hills, a glimpse of the Tiber, of sunshine savagely bright on camellias. She delighted in the press and the noise. An old man offered her a seat and was disappointed when she refused his offer. She liked the jumble of languages.

They went on talking, joking, laughing, all those people on their way into the centre of Rome. Maggie bent again to try and see out a window. Roman ruins slid by above the roofs of speeding cars. Terme di Caracalla. The heaped ruins. The collapsed attics.

At the Termini she hauled her bags into a queue and took a cab to the Fenix Hotel on Viale Gorizia. Ida and Josie weren't in their room; Fish wasn't in his either, but he had reserved a room for her. She went up to her room and lay down to have a nap and fell into a deep sleep in which she dreamt passionately of me, Jack Deemer.

In her dream she and I were in the bathroom in the tower in Inez's house, and when she asked me to make love I bent headlong into the healing water, I was the foam-fresh lover she had only dreamed. The tongue too has its sense of smell. The herbs of the sea. The coral tips of her nipples. I followed my lashing tongue; her foregone lovers fell like weeds.

When the knock at the door awakened her she could or would not quite free herself from sleep. The excited voices, sounding so far away, she realized after a while, were those of Josie and Ida.

Maggie was completely dressed. She had fallen back across the bed after taking off her shoes. Now she eased herself up onto the edge of her bed, onto her feet.

Ida and Josie burst through the opened door.

"You're here," Josie said, waiting her turn to hug Maggie. "You're really here." Then it was Ida who was talking. "Get your shoes on. It's our coffee time."

Maggie wasn't allowed the small renewal that a shower would afford. She used the bathroom, brushed her teeth, found her travellers' cheques. She dropped her key at the desk. Outside on the street they signalled a taxi and bustled into it, Ida giving the driver instructions. They were in too much of a hurry to wait for a bus.

They got out of the taxi near the Piazza della Rotonda. Rome was a blast of afternoon light. Josie and Ida led the way past a sidewalk artist who was kneeling on the pavement, chalk in hand, his hands the many colours of the chalk sticks he used. He was colouring a huge bird, bright red flames at its breast. He knelt dumbly on the pavement of the piazza, between the Rameses I's obelisk and the eighteen granite pillars of the Pantheon, seemingly lost in concentration. But he turned his head to acknowledge the coins that Josie and Ida dropped between his upturned bare feet.

They walked into the small maze of outdoor tables, Maggie following, and found a table.

"Our table," Ida said. "This is where it happened . . ."

"Ice cream?" The waiter bowed to the two old women.

Ida replied for all of them. "*Gelati.*"

"*Si,* Josie said. "*Gelato.*"

The waiter bowed again.

Josie asked what flavour Maggie would have, then said to the waiter, "*Uno tutti fruiti.* Two *chocolati.*"

Ida was impatient to explain. "Sitting right there where you're sitting now." She paused as if Maggie must stand up and look at the chair she had sat on. "It was him."

"Manny," Josie said. "He was sitting right here at our table at our coffee time."

Maggie held her tongue.

"He spoke to us. In English. We understood everything he said."

These two women saw Papa B's puppet, Maggie decided, balancing her elbows on the small round table, then decided that any dwarf under high heaven must be Manny. She should have gone straight to Greece to talk to Henry about his claim to have hit on fortune itself. He had connected — that was his word — with a collection of icons and needed her advice — one of his words that translated freely as, help, please help me, hurry.

"So what did he say?"

"He said, 'Excuse me.' Very politely."

Josie added her agreement. "He was the picture of politeness."

"That's all he said? 'Excuse me.'"

"It was the way he said it that mattered. He looked me right in the eye." Ida stared into Maggie's eyes by way of demonstration. "Apparently he hadn't ordered. He looked us over. Both of us. His eyes are a dream. Then he up and left."

"Polite as pie," Josie said, to Maggie. "He just hopped off that chair you're sitting on and he was gone. Slick and clean out of sight. Try to follow that man in this crowd."

Maggie despaired. She had been tempted to believe the two old women when they phoned her. Or perhaps she had been so desperate to escape from Papa B that she would have believed anything.

"I thought Fish might show up." Maggie must talk to him, find out if he believed Josie and Ida. She should have insisted on talking to him before deciding to stop in Rome.

"Fish? You'll be lucky if we see him at the hotel tonight." Ida was always defending someone or other. "He's a busy man."

"Tomorrow — Tivoli. Just be patient." Josie was looking around expectantly, watching everyone except Maggie and Ida as she spoke. "Fish says they treat ailments like mine and Ida's. It might be good for you too, Maggie."

"Fish has connections," Ida explained.

Maggie picked the wafer off her dish of ice cream and at the same time ordered cappuccino. She was stalling. Against her own better judgement, she was waiting for the ghost of Dr De Medeiros to put in an appearance. She was hoping. Hello, she would say, nice of you to show up. What's the idea, deceiving old ladies?

She looked out over the artist at work on his firebird: inside the Pantheon, she remembered, you could look straight up and see overhead a round hole in the sky. The perfect escape.

Ida and Josie finished their ice cream and decided that after all they would have cappuccino. They wanted Manny De Medeiros to surprise Maggie. They were counting on him; he had not, they were certain, shown up at their special table by accident. They argued with Maggie. Maggie fiddled for a long time with the bill, then paid, then waited for her change, then delayed again while she figured out what coins to leave on the table.

"What's the hurry?" Ida said. "We have all day."

They moved off, stopping at a little postcard shop around the corner so Maggie could buy cards. She could send them back with Josie and Ida and in that way avoid Inez Catonio's private eye. She wanted to send cryptic messages to Papa B and to Bludgett; messages on the backs of cards that said more than did her words. She found two cards, both of a painting by Rothko, *Untitled.* She would write on the cards later. He is not to be found. Ghost fails to show.

They moved slowly through the crowd, onto a street marked SENSO UNICO. They walked with the hundreds of other pedestrians, not on the impossibly narrow sidewalk, but in the roadway. Maggie walked ahead, the two old women following after. The bus stop was near, they insisted; they could take a bus back to the hotel.

The limousine that bore down on Maggie took her completely by surprise, swinging into the one-way street in the wrong direction. She had only time to flatten herself against a wall.

A moment later the limousine was gone, Ida and Josie were at Maggie's side, solicitous, protective.

"Did you see that?" Maggie said.

Other people crowded around, indignant, asking Maggie if she had been injured, then asking Josie and Ida.

Maggie was more shocked than hurt. "Did you see the man in the back of that car? That was the dwarf."

"You're imagining things," Ida said. "The back seat was empty."

"It was that Manny fellow," Maggie said. "The spitting image of Papa B's Manny. You could tell by his hair."

Josie tried to placate Maggie. "I saw the car, Maggie. The driver was so huge he could hardly see out the window. That's what happened."

Josie led the way toward a bus stop while Ida, following after, gave support to Maggie. She tried to limp but couldn't decide which leg it was that felt the pain.

Remembering later she realized it was Fish, not she, who next morning over a late breakfast of rolls and coffee downstairs in the hotel suggested they go first to the Villa d'Este. Ida and Josie were eager to get to the Tivoli spa. Maggie sided with Fish, voting to see the huge garden that had survived since the Renaissance. "It's full of fountains," Fish assured Josie and Ida. "You'll like it. We'll get to the spa when the sun is at its hottest."

They took a bus from Rome to Tivoli. But Fish began to waver, getting off the bus near the Villa d'Este. He suggested they stop somewhere for cappuccino.

"Let's get a wiggle on," Josie told him. She was anxious to visit the spa. "My garden must be nothing but weeds by now."

"I forgot to check," Maggie said. "I forgot to tell Thomas —"

Ida covered for her. "Maggie is all shook up. Let's go wherever she wants to go. Except into the path of a limousine."

Fish led the way crookedly among stalls where hawkers offered for sale shining leather purses, ice cream, film, postcards, whole banks of ladies' leather shoes, T-shirts, flowers. Josie wanted to stop and watch an artist carving a cameo from a seashell; Ida caught her elbow and hurried her along.

They dodged through groups of tourists and found the entrance to the cardinal's garden.

"You've been here before?" Ida said to Fish, marvelling at the way he manoeuvred his way through the crowd.

"I was here yesterday. And the day before."

Josie disapproved. "Mr. Deemer sent you here to study spas, not gardens."

"This will be good food for what ails you," Fish said. "A sixteenth-century garden. The greatest of them all. You'll love it."

They lined up to pay their five thousand lires each for a *biglietto d'ingresso*. Fish bought four tickets, then led the way into the courtyard of the villa. He was nervous, more in a hurry than the three women. "Begun in 1550. Dedicated to Hippolytus, if I remember correctly —"

"You were here yesterday," Josie said. "You should remember correctly."

"Begun by the last of the great Renaissance cardinals, when he was hardly Maggie's age." Fish was talking,

Maggie sensed, to hide his unease. He hardly paused to look around. "I was given a tour. Nothing makes me forget like a tour."

Josie stopped dead, unwilling to move. "Look. It's wonderful. It's perfect."

Maggie tugged at Josie's arm. "You haven't seen it yet."

They had no time for the cobbled courtyard and the stone arches fronting the shaded walkway. Ida and Josie wanted to see the fountains. It was Ida who led the way from the terrace down a long flight of stairs to the avenue below, then to another flight of stairs, then to the first sloping path. Josie tried to correct Ida; they'd missed a turn, they were losing the crowds of tourists.

"It's a horse with wings on it," Ida said. "You should have brought your camera, Josie."

On a rock in the circular pool in front of them stood a statue of Pegasus, the great winged horse rearing on its hind legs, a stream of water like a stiletto rising between its raised front legs.

"What next," Josie said. "Where do they find this stuff?"

"A collector," Fish said, to Maggie. He was leading the way now. "A great collector, Cardinal Ippolito."

"So is Jack Deemer," Ida said, overhearing Fish. "And just imagine the junk he owns. I'm surprised he hasn't bought this place."

Ida was my champion at times, in her unwitting way. Maggie, on the other hand, was flat out in her admiration of the famous cardinal. She could love a man like that. She liked his name. Cardinal Ippolito II d'Este. She liked his collecting for his garden from the ruins left by that other collector, Hadrian, who collected from the Greeks, who collected from the Egyptians, who had in turn come up with a collection of winged animals of their own from God knows where. There are horses and there are horses. I have my two collections of saddles, one from the Argentine, one from Mexico. I have my treasured collection of riding boots and of lariats.

Ida would admire at least some of my collections. Gold thimbles. Singletrees and doubletrees. Samurai armour. Codpieces from all over Europe. Darning needles. Devices for the carding of wool. All my four warehouses crammed with collections from around this spinning top we call a globe. And Dorf once acquired for me a collection of children's tops from a Chinese man in Singapore who had killed a man in Thailand in order to get them. Collectors too are collected, as I well know. Julie Magnuson taught me that much. She, or her sidekick —

They saw him there.

Josie saw him first. She saw the small man on the parapet of a pool so large it seemed a small lake. Behind him was the towering stone bowl from whose rim a cascade fell as a rainbowed curtain. The Oval Fountain. Tourists, behind that watery curtain, walked a stone ledge and laughed and shuddered.

The dwarf was standing up straight on the parapet in front of the pool. The parapet was yellow and green and white in its pattern of majolica tiles. Behind the dwarf, on either side of the cascade, water nymphs set in niches in the stone arcade poured each a stream of water from a stone pitcher, into the mirroring lake.

It was Ida who went forward as if she must catch the dwarf before he flung himself into the arms of his own image in the water. It seemed he might plunge in and be lost, out of all reach.

The tourists nearest him drew back.

Dr Manuel De Medeiros had the gall to bow. He made a flourish that was at once a welcome and an introduction to his luminous and assuring presence. He was on stage. The grand motion of his small right arm was a teasing invitation.

"Good health," he said.

It was his gesture that irritated Maggie. She wanted to rush forward and push the man into the pool. He stood there, eloquent and silent, his long blond hair unruffled by his deep bow. He had on a pale blue silk shirt that was alive with gold thread. He had on blue silk slacks, rolled high enough to show his bare feet.

His shoes, absurdly small, were perched like two curious yellow birds beside his bare feet on the narrow ledge that surrounded the pool.

De Medeiros, balanced there with the cascade and the water nymphs behind him, was slightly more handsome than Maggie had expected. Papa B's puppet had made the doctor clumsy and sullen. Yet he was elegantly confident in every gesture. He was, Maggie told herself in that instant, not a man who would stumble overboard from a shuddering canoe. He was amused, deliberate, yet concerned. He had been waiting. He was confident that he could deliver.

Dr Manuel De Medeiros sat down on the parapet and slipped his yellow leather shoes onto his bare feet without socks. He turned, then, and let himself off the stone ledge as if he might be climbing out of a sarcophagus. I make this obvious comparison because it was he who, before his own supposed death, and with only a little prodding from me, arranged to have my wife's coffin shipped to my Calgary home.

He turned as if to walk away and disappear into the crowd or in among the ancient trees or in behind the many shoulders and edges of mossy stone.

The tourists, feeling they were entitled at least to a jest or a song from a dwarf, went back to their guide books. Maggie and Fish and Ida and Josie were alone in following after the silent man. They fell in behind him as if they were gigantic children brought to watch in that treacherous garden for a rare blossom or a rare bird. They glanced around, distrusting the gravel pathways, the bushes, the garrulous speech of the fountains.

They had entered onto the mosaic walkway of the Viale delle Cento Fontane. The Pathway of the Hundred Fountains. Over De Medeiros's blond head they could see on their left the three long rows of fountains that teased the silence with their music. The stone obelisks and boats and the fleur-de-lis shot water straight into the air. The stone eagles, spaced in that row of fountains, seemed intent on guarding the myriad streams that fell from the highest channel down through moss and maidenhair ferns to a second channel, then through gaping animal mouths to a channel at the level of the walkway.

No one would speak; it would seem a folly to speak to the dead. Good health, he had said. As if addressing a congress of the insane. No one had been able to say in return so much as, the same to you.

De Medeiros did not deign to glance back. He only stopped when he came, on his right, to a small stone sphinx on a pedestal of brick and moss. The sphinx had full breasts that were fountains. De Medeiros had hardly to bend; he put his mouth to a stone breast and drank.

"Hope it loosens his tongue," Josie whispered to Ida.

"Wish it was rye and ginger," Ida said.

De Medeiros looked up from the stone breast. He smiled. His teeth were small, meticulous. The one tooth in gold, under the thin line of his almost invisible moustache, seemed only then to have appeared in his mouth.

He led the way down the Stairs of the Bubbling Fountains. On either side of the long stairway a sequence of basins topped the balustrades. A flower of water bubbled into a cup, fell away into a basin the shape of a sarcophagus, bubbled again into a cup, fell away into a stuccoed basin, bubbled again, fell again, bubbled again, fell again, bubbled —

Maggie followed, words tripping over each other in her mind. Bollori. Pergola. Fontanel. Obelisk. It was Fish she heard. He was talking softly, as if in a cemetery, telling her about the garden. Fish liked gardens. Deadman Spring was a garden because of his attention. He wanted this place too, this occasion, to be a part of his care, and he could only care now by talking softly to Maggie. Espalier and box hedge. It was as if the appearance of De Medeiros was of no interest whatsoever to him. He was marvelling instead at the tens of thousands of flowering plants and shrubs and ornamental trees. Centuries of planning and planting, of neglect and decay, of replanting and grooming and reshaping. The geometry of paths, the architecture of water. Fish had somewhere in his past been an engineer. He wanted to tell Maggie about the magic worked here with water, but she would hardly listen. This magnificent world, he was trying to tell her. It was his gift to her, his warning, his apology. The theft of hundreds of statues, to fill the garden, the theft of those statues from the garden. But water went on shaping the trees fresh, the stone new.

They had come to the fish ponds. De Medeiros, as if everlastingly drawn to the flat, mysterious surface of water, stopped where three huge fish ponds, rectangular, framed in stone, lay before him. He moved to the edge of the centre pond as if he intended, once again, before their eyes, as he had done before the eyes of Dorf, to disappear.

Ars topiaria, Fish was saying. Typology, he told her; you have to realize, the garden for them was a book. He sounded like Henry. He sounded like Thomas Bludgett. She realized that Fish had spent his days and years reading about gardens and had never quite looked at a garden. Lucullus, he was saying; his villa provided the model. Read Vitruvius. Read Plinius. Maggie could have hated him then, for his sounding like Henry, Henry going on about his icons, not glancing up at the icon on the wall. Fish would not let the garden whisper in at her eyes. The geometry of the garden, Fish was saying. This, he whispered, is something Jack Deemer can't collect. There is a limit, finally, to what Jack Deemer can collect, even if he believes he can collect everything, including this, including us. The geometry of the garden was lost for centuries, and then it was found again, in the Quattrocento villa. Fish wasn't speaking to her at all, he was speaking to himself, as Thomas Bludgett spoke to himself, as Manny De Medeiros, staring into the centre pool, into the pool that might or might not have in it myriad fish, might be talking to himself. The icons of Theophanes the Cretan, Henry said to her. But he was saying it to himself. The face of God, he said, to her, to himself; I want an icon of the face of God. Read Boccaccio, Fish was telling her. After the castle, the rediscovery of the garden. Fish was making sense of the world for her, and she couldn't follow anything he said. Read, he was telling her. Read Leon Battista Alberti. Read Martini. Maggie wanted him to tell her to look at the garden, but he was telling her to look at books. *Obiter dictum*, she wanted to tell him.

But they weren't at the fish ponds now, they were walking. Maggie wished with all her nerve ends for a cigarette. She wanted to inhale, hold, exhale. She was listening to Fish and watching De Medeiros and thinking of the cigarettes she'd left hidden behind the dusty dinner plates in her kitchen. In George's kitchen. And what if George returned while she was gone? She hadn't allowed for that. The string that was meant to guide you free might just as easily tangle your feet.

They were surrounded by cypress trees. Good old death, Maggie thought, tells me about the cypress, Fish. Leave it to Manny to bring us here.

"Orpheus," Fish was saying, whispering. "Went to hell — and came back claiming a cypress marks the spot where you do your forgetting. Stay away from the waters of forgetfulness. Don't drink that stuff, madam."

Maggie whispered in return, "Make mine scotch with a little bit of water."

As she spoke, Manny stepped away from the circular marbled floor of the centre of the Rotonda dei Cipressi. Ida and Josie, then Fish and Maggie too, trailed after him as he moved into the paths made by orange trees and cherry trees and elms and figs.

They made a turn, and another, into the labyrinth of flowering trees and sculpted hedges. The walls directing them were leafy and green. Maggie did not want to escape. She fell behind the others, trying to close her ears against the consolation that Fish offered with his words. She was tempted to take her own turn; she would disappear, in under the shadows of the cypress trees.

But they had come to a statue. The statue was set into a grotto that was in turn set close and protective against a high stone wall.

Maggie at first saw the high head, regal, crowned with a crown that seemed the tower of a castle. Only as she tried to gauge her own wonder did she let register in her mind the figure's many breasts. They were ranked and multiplied, the travertine breasts; they were sculpted in stone that had grown in water; they were touched green with moss. Each nipple gave down a jet of water.

The face was patiently serene. The statue's right hand was missing. The statue's left hand was large, opened in a gesture of giving. The breasts were full, large-nippled, abundant, giving down a rain of water into a pool.

Josie laughed with delight. Ida swore a soft oath of wonder.

Maggie, glancing away from the figure of the goddess, noticed the high walls on either side of the stuccoed grotto, the stone patched ragged with stucco. She looked again to the statue and its wide abundance of marble breasts, the gleaming white jets of water, and she did not see where Julie Magnuson came from.

I had wanted her dead; I've confessed that too. I've told you that, if not in one way, then in another. I had wanted her stone-cold dead. I took a peek into her coffin, just to make sure.

The body had not been found for many days, there in the heat of the Algarve, there in a Mercedes Benz that was caught like a child's kite, high in a cork oak tree. Dr De Medeiros called long distance at his own expense to tell me that.

The accident, he said, had demolished the body. It was, he said, a sight too horrible for a loving husband's eyes.

I was alone with the casket when I opened it. That cost me a pretty penny too, that privacy. It cost me a good deal more than the preacher who married me to Julie Magnuson on the morning of her announced wedding day. The good doctor had shipped the casket from Portugal, complete with a notarized letter that announced the finding of the body, the unspeakable decay, the doctor's unspeakable grief and his understanding of my own. I should have recognized in that, Julie Magnuson's style.

Her casket was empty. Except for some carefully distributed lead weights. For four years I lived a kind of death. I lived the death that waiting is.

Julie and her dear doctor were standing there, together, side by side, in front of the Fountain of Diana of Ephesus.

Diana. Artemis. Call the goddess what you will. She was, in any case, stolen from her place on the coast of Asia Minor where she ruled in majesty, and blood, for centuries. Some collectors resort to theft. Butcher, the Spartans called her. She-Bear. She was Ursa Major to some. She nurtured everything that lived. What kind of collecting is that?

Fish, all his life, was in love with Julie. I was never deceived about that. He was using those two old women, Ida and Josie. He was using Maggie too, but she was blinded by her own words.

Manny De Medeiros was standing like a post in front of the pool in front of Diana. Like a proud post, if a post can be proud. He was a dwarf, of course. But he had the swagger about him of a man who would pretend to heal the whole world of its ills. And there, in front of that statue, standing beside Julie, he was as motionless as a post. As motionless as a cypress.

I suppose I will always be in love with Julie. I've explained that to Maggie. She laughs and says I will always be in love with whatever it is that I haven't been able to add to my collection of collections.

It was Julie who did the talking, there in the cardinal's garden, in front of the cardinal's pagan statue. She turned away from the statue, toward the little crowd of worshippers who stood in dumb obeisance. She spoke two sentences, carefully, with the intention of hurting Maggie. She wanted to hurt Maggie, of that I have no doubt. Maggie insists the remarks — let down like drops of water by a Chinese torturer — were meant for my absent and innocent head. I disagree.

"It's about my wedding dress," Julie said, "I've come."

14

Love and perversity are too often twins.

Julie Magnuson and Manny together had conspired to fake her death, the two of them plotting, making ghostly what she and I had created. I expect Julie picked out the Portuguese coffin that was sent to me, there in Calgary where I awaited her return; Manny was hardly a master of good taste. They staged their disappearances, the two of them; they were staging their return.

It was Julie's blunt announcement that made Maggie Wilder decide to call Papa B. The remark about the wedding dress was unnerving for Maggie. One might have expected a show of regret at the deception practised, even a brief apology. But we have so few ceremonies, so few handy speeches, for those who came back from wherever.

Maggie could not immediately get to a phone because everyone was busy heaping varieties of praise on the reappeared Julie Magnuson. She was as disturbing and attractive as she had always been, though I was not there to add my admonitions along with my praise. The reference to the wedding dress, needless to say, rang bells of discord all around. I was in Calgary waiting for my phone to ring; Karen Strike was at Deadman Spring waiting to hear from Fish. Fish, instead of calling anyone, was once again, as he had been for most of his miserable life, worshipping at the feet of his clay idol.

Julie did that to men. And to women too, for that matter. She persuaded them to worship. She was beautiful, yes, but, as Maggie described her to me later, she was also cool, severe, demanding, presumptuous, arrogant. And yet, for all that, I delighted to lie in her arms, kissing one breast, then the other, then the first again, then the other, until I fell asleep. "My little collector," she sometimes called me, fondly watching. In a feigning of greed I sometimes pressed her nipples close together, determined to take both at once into my hungry mouth.

Her admirers at the time saw her imperious side but didn't have enough sense to be cautious. Ida and Josie were falling all over themselves and making preposterous statements, to puzzled tourists, to the surrounding trees I suppose, about people coming back from the dead.

Josie was struck by Julie's height. Julie had a deceiving way of standing tall. She claimed she picked up this manner from walking with Fish, when they were — as the phrase had it then — courting. But in fact I always felt it was intended to intimidate me, for while I am at least of average height, and nothing resembling a dwarf, I am a fraction of an inch shorter than she.

She was wearing bright green shoes with impossibly high heels for the occasion. It was Ida who noticed that detail. The paths in the cardinal's garden were not intended for high heels, but that made no difference to Julie. She made the rules and expected the world to accommodate itself.

I seem to be avoiding the essential matter. Julie Magnuson, presumed dead, was back to life and apparently fit as a fiddle. Further, she was still under the illusion that I had intended her death when I paid Dr De Medeiros a handsome sum to treat her in the spa in Portugal that was possibly the spa I most sought to find in the wide world.

Maggie, feeling both depressed and elated, instead of asking herself why that dangerous woman had *really* chosen that time to make her reappearance, found some weak excuse to run back to the palace. She was on the phone in a jiffy, thanks to those horrors called credit cards. And I might say I have never in my whole life bothered to own one. But where was I, yes —

I had expected for four rather distressing years that Julie Magnuson might be prowling the night like an angry ghost in search of a respectable grave. I had not peeked into her coffin for nothing, on the day of her burial; I had counted the small lead weights, so carefully arranged in the box that had cost me a king's ransom. We all love her, you understand. Those of us who are still alive are still in love with her.

It was Bludgett who answered Maggie's feverish call.

"Thomas?"

"Maggie? Why are you calling at this ungodly hour?"

"I assumed you'd be awake."

"Your friend Papa B has got me playing doll house with him. I'm taking up puppetry. For the past two days I've been trying to handle four puppet rods with two hands. I should have been born with three."

"Thomas. Listen. Stop. I want to talk to Papa B."

"You told me to keep him in the attic. It isn't difficult. I'm surprised he can make it to the bathroom on his own. I thought I might get him a potty chair."

"Please, Thomas. Call him to the phone."

"I doubt that he'll obey."

"Don't be smart, Thomas. Tell him it's about Julie Magnuson."

"— — —"

"You heard me. Julie Magnuson."

Bludgett was gone then. Maggie thinking, I could hang up. I could hang up the receiver now, before it's too late. Let Bludgett climb the stairs until he's hollering at the moon. What time is it there? Two grown men, one unwilling to sleep, the other unable to sleep. Let Papa B decide to run his questions through his puppets a million more times, looking for the one mutation, the one small, impossible variation —

But that variation had occurred. They had decided to die, Manny and Julie. They had tried it. And the experiment on the whole had put them off the project. They had come begging their way back to life, in a Renaissance cardinal's garden. In a garden full of tourists. They were back, and all they wanted, they said, was cappuccino and gelati with people who might be called friends, a yawn and a stretch in the noonday light, a bit of gossip about what had happened to old acquaintances in the four years they were away.

Living is a habit that is hard to break. It was not the wonder of Julie's return that filled her little pod of admirers with delight, but rather her wanting to have a chair to sit on and a cup to lift to her wide and almost smiling mouth. She wanted first of all, she said, to take Josie and Ida for the swim they'd been promised. That set the whole lot to scampering toward the gate. How Manny managed to tag along I won't so much as ask.

"Hello?"

Maggie hated the way Papa B had of saying hello. His voice was listening for itself to respond instead of responding to another.

"Dorf," Maggie said. She didn't like calling him that. She used the name he had been given by me, by Jack Deemer. That was the name she challenged him with, even when her intention was to deliver good news. "You're the free man you used to be."

Dorf fell totally silent. Maggie's impossible statement silenced Dorf. Its philosophic implications were enough to make a deaf man complain of the noise. How free did any of us used to be? I, for instance, slaved and sweated to acquire a fortune beyond my own mathematic, and in the process fastened my failing gaze on love. I refuse to live only to die. Some nights I rehearse immortality by examining my collection of cartridges.

Dorf responded by holding his breath, then ventured, exhaling as he did so, "You're in Rome?"

Maggie wanted, basically, to bite his ear.

"I'm in Tivoli. I'm just outside —" She couldn't remember the name of the garden. "Julie Magnuson is here. She and Manny are here. Together."

Take that, she thought. Listen to that, and then, if you are able, go on being silent. Did you hear what I just said? Now draw one large deep breath — and hold it until the cows come home.

She had added the word *together* she realized, as a conniving gesture that might stop him from seizing his freedom. She wanted the word to curdle his mind.

She wanted him to die of astonishment. She listened with bitter pleasure for the thud of his brand-new corpse onto the worn linoleum of cousin George's everlastingly chilly, damp, messy, mouldy kitchen. She thought of the four calendars, as indifferent as snakes in a winter den, failing to record so much as the year of his demise.

"Then she isn't dead," Dorf said.

Maggie wanted him to explode from his own denseness. She wanted to place in his clever hands a bomb of such exquisite complexity and workmanship that he couldn't help caressing it while it exploded in his face. It was his infernal damned clever hands that made him a puppeteer, a craftsman, a shaper, a lover, a collector's agent. She thought of his careful fingers, stilled by the telephone receiver.

"Try to get hold of this," Maggie said. "I'm in a hurry. This is costing me money. She is here. Julie Magnuson. She is here. Alive."

"I'll come there then." Dorf said.

"Papa B," Maggie said. "Dorf. You can't come here."

"Why can't I?" he asked, his innocence as appalling as ever.

Maggie had no answer.

"I'll make arrangements," Dorf said.

The telephone line crackled. The sound of cracking ice filled the receiver that Maggie held away from her ear. She noticed the flash of light on her wedding ring. She hadn't noticed her wedding ring in weeks. Why was she bothering to wear it? She would go into Rome and catch a flight to Siphnos. Henry wanted her to come to Greece, he'd found an adequate pair of rooms on a perfect island where she could spend her days and nights writing the perfect account of the life she had neglected to live. Henry's irony was as predictable as his morning stool.

And that unfathomable calamity had been visited upon her too. The epigrammatic insult of the vanished ring. When she told Henry, one afternoon at the Parthenon, that she was about to go out and track the life she had failed to follow when she or it took an unexpected turn, he responded by gaping. He gaped. He stood either in mockery or disbelief with his mouth wide open. And Maggie yanked the ring off her ring finger and hurled it at the gaping man and happened to hurl it into his gaping mouth. He swallowed. He gulped, and in gulping he swallowed Maggie's wedding ring. And then for four days, each morning, in a cheap and foul-smelling hotel in Athens — each morning for four days — the two of them together, lovingly side by side, bent over the toilet bowl and poked through Henry's perfectly formed if somewhat too dry stool. His turd. His shit. They poked and prodded and waited and hoped as if the excrement of the famous if largely unpublished professor of Byzantine icons must contain the absolute and unspeakable truth.

"Good luck," Maggie said. She was, with the thumb and forefinger of her right hand, removing the wedding band from the ring finger on the hand that held the phone. Delicately, without glancing down, she dropped the ring into the mess of cigarette butts and discarded tickets at her feet. "I'm going to Greece. To the island of Siphnos."

Dorf didn't respond. He wasn't interested, apparently, in what she might be doing. That too offended her. She struck at him, insisted on saying what he didn't have the courtesy to hear. She knew without having to stop to think that William William Dorfendorf, released into freedom, would lapse into his pathetic need to run around collecting collections for the man who had been determined to kill him. Even habit is a habit.

"I'm joining Henry there. He's on the track of a collection of icons that's about to be shipped from Mount Athos."

"Mount Athos?" Papa B said. "Icons are never shipped from Mount Athos."

"These icons are being shipped from Mount Athos. Henry has phoned me three times to say so."

"Icons never leave Mount Athos. The mountain itself will leave Mount Athos before any icons leave Mount Athos."

Maggie heard his interest and forgot about Henry's swearing her to silence and secrecy. She liked Dorf's unease. She had stirred him into responding to something and that in itself was a victory.

"He's buying them. He and two Greek guys. He phoned me just today before I was out of bed. He has clinched the deal. He needs my assistance. We're going to use our house and our savings —"

Maggie, thinking to herself, Julie Magnuson has returned from the other side of whatever a grave is and here we are, Dorf and I, playing still the old game of domestic tyranny.

"They must be hot," Dorf said. "Stolen. I'd steer clear if I were you, Maggie." And then he added, "Do you know where Julie is staying?"

"I have no idea." Maggie hung up the phone.

How I found out about the collection of icons from Mount Athos is a curious story. I don't collect a whole lot of collections of art; I find them somewhat trivial. I do have a couple of Picassos, but then, who doesn't?

Manuel De Medeiros was a spa doctor, and even on the day of Julie Magnuson's malicious return to the so-called world, he could do only what spa doctors do.

They went, the whole lot of them, in Manny's limousines, to the Tivoli spa. Ida and Josie imagined themselves on the verge of instant cures.

Manny had two limousines, both black and large. He kept a clientele, it turned out, in a number of spas, including Montecatini and Tivoli, where the sick go to be cured and the rich go to be rich. The two limousines were driven by men who were twins. They were identical, large, monstrous twins, each with one eye and one eye patch, both dressed in black suits, white shirts and black ties. Fortunately, one was blind in the left eye, one in the right.

The two limousines and their twin drivers and their passengers headed straight for the Terme Acque Albule. While the pools were officially closed, waiting for the season to begin, for the famous doctor and his friends they were unofficially open. Dr De Medeiros, in his slightly officious way, led his little throng of followers directly to the largest of the five pools. Ida and Josie sniffed the sulphurous waters and started to undress. They had once or twice, the two old women, ventured near St. Peter's and the Vatican Museum and the Colosseum. They had each morning gone into the centre of Rome on a number 60 bus to have coffee and ice cream in their favourite piazza while they decided what to do in the afternoon. And each afternoon they had, after the expenditure of so much energy, stayed in their hotel room and had a small nip and slept.

At last they had travelled the thirty kilometres to Tivoli and had, via the detour to the cardinal's garden, arrived at the spa. They took off their clothes right there under a solitary palm, with Maggie holding up a large white towel to give them privacy. They put on bathing suits that were surely collectors' items. They let the stark Italian sun snap at their pale shoulders; they let themselves sink deep into the mineral waters, under the scouring heat of the Italian May afternoon. They recalled with shivers of delight the rains they had left behind. Josie, her mouth almost under water, inhaled the vapours into her troubled lungs. Ida raised her large hands out of the water and flexed them open and shut and plunged them again into the water, persuaded that her old knuckles were newly hinged.

Julie Magnuson, watching, began to undress. Fish and Maggie had already got into their swimsuits. Julie took her own good time. In order to wet so much as a big toe, she had to be stark naked. Obviously, she hadn't been hiding in the dark; she was tanned from the eyelids of her green eyes to her green toenail polish. Revealing her body had never been a problem for Julie. "Ida and Josie are wearing enough swimsuit for all of us," she explained, when poor Fish almost drowned himself trying at once to watch and to look away.

Ida and Josie, their visit to the spa about to end on the day it began, followed Julie's lead — as if being naked must be part of the cure. The doctor's magic was to hit them direct. They stripped right down to their birthday suits; splashing and shouting and laughing, they began to have the time of their lives. They dared Fish, who somewhere on the journey had been persuaded to take off his toque, revealing a balding head, to take off his swimsuit as well.

"No way," Fish said.

It was the last day of the vacation for those two women. They were to fly home in the morning. The attention they received from Dr De Medeiros was a special gift, possibly a thank you. He walked around the pool in his unlikely costume, saying little to anyone, muttering to himself, assuming his very presence would heal and anoint a limb or a lung. And Ida and Josie believed him, right down to the base of each callus and corn.

"Dr De Medeiros can't swim," Ida said, speaking to Josie.

Julie Magnuson winked at both of them. "Only like a fish. You should see him."

Fish, listening, allowed himself a smile. Perhaps he recognized I had in my own way done him a favour, saving him from a fate worse than death. She was not without her malevolent side, as I was again, and soon, to discover.

One is not likely to amass a fortune and then collect collections without making an enemy or two. Fish, listening to the conversation that hot afternoon in the mineral waters of the Tivoli spa, as usual resolved to turn tail and run. First, he took off his swimsuit and tossed it out of the pool. Then, using his hands as fig leaves, he announced he would fly back to Vancouver with Ida and Josie. He proclaimed, having no more than glanced around that famous spa, that his work was finished. And I had put up the money for his trip.

Fish hated me, for whatever reasons, and yet I gave him a job, I kept him from encountering his own failure by making him caretaker of my spa at Deadman

Spring. He had lost his ability to work as an engineer; he was at best a handyman, fixing a valve that wasn't working, monitoring water temperatures. Tinkering with a pump. Tending the lawns and the bushes. But gratitude is rarer than gold. I have, somewhere in one of my warehouses in Calgary, a large collection of gold bracelets, each made in the form of a snake swallowing its own tail.

Somehow it was their being naked that set the gang in the pool to talking about the wedding dress.

If you ask me, Fish was the culprit. He and Julie and Manny had been in cahoots all along. Why not make matters worse for me, if they possibly could? Fish, pretending to work for me — and pretending to work was as close as he ever got — had all the while been Julie's lackey, listening in and watching out, waiting for the shift of a grain of sand that would bring down the mountain. And then the wedding dress spoke itself.

I was not there to defend my reputation, so naturally I was pictured as the villain. Julie Magnuson told all those people in the Tivoli spa that I had not married her at all; I had collected her. And to make that clear, I had sent back the dress she got married in.

We were distinguished lovers, Julie and I. How lovers proceed with each and each is always a mystery to others.

Maggie had stayed in her swimsuit and out of the water. She was sitting on the edge of the pool, her feet and ankles in the mineral waters. Sitting there with that motley crew, she had Dorf on her mind. We had not yet met, she and I; she was no doubt considering

Dorf's curious remarks about Henry's collection of icons.

"I never want to lay eyes on Jack Deemer," Julie said. "Never again. Not ever."

"He couldn't stand that," Fish said. "That's the one thing he couldn't stand. Not seeing you. Now that you're back."

It was then that Maggie said she might leave next day. Or at least the day after. She said she would see Ida and Josie to the airport, then talk to an airline agent while she was there; she would find out what it would cost her to change her ticket.

Maggie wanted to ask about me, and in her strange way of proceeding she began instead to speak of Henry. "I'll leave on the first available flight that goes to Athens. I'll take the ferry from Piraeus to the islands."

Perhaps she understood, in some oblique way, that what she wanted above all else was to protect my life. The wedding dress was a kind of prognostication. It was not at all what Julie thought it was.

Everyone wanted to know why Maggie was in such a rush to be off to Siphnos.

"Henry Ketch could buy a collection of icons one day and misplace it the next. He's an idiot savant without the savant part."

Ida and Josie were signalling that she should mention Papa B. Maggie had that to contend with, on top of everything else.

"What icons are those?" De Medeiros asked.

There is something static about icons that appeals to me. Progress is an illusion that icons refuse, and I cherish them for that. Papa B, in his enthusiasm for puppets and their trumped-up stories, kept on hoping for the best. But look at the famous icons. Pick one at random, if you will. *St Cosmas the Healer. St Orestis.* Look at any diptych of your choice. Not oil but rather tempera. Tempera on great, thick slabs of wood. A different light and a different promise. Consider *The Raising of Lazarus*, once a part of an altar screen on Mount Athos, now somewhere in Athens, a part of a private collection. Let sleeping dogs lie, the icons say; leave bad enough alone.

Maggie slipped into the water. She kept on her swimsuit, but she slipped into the pool nevertheless, and then there was no stopping her tongue. Ida and Josie waited for the revelation: Dorf is alive and well and hiding. They winked and waited. And then they accepted Maggie's wisdom; they went back to the attention that Manny offered, back to the mineral waters and his abrupt and miraculous cures.

Fish, listening to Maggie, saw his chance. He said, jokingly, to Ida and Josie, "Now don't you two go tell Karen Strike there's a collection of icons floating loose. She'll be in Greece in a flash. And God knows who she might have with her."

Manny, who had not appeared to be listening, picked up on the joke. "Better still — please do tell her. I beg you."

15

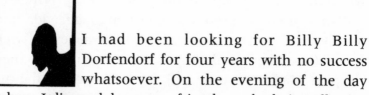

I had been looking for Billy Billy Dorfendorf for four years with no success whatsoever. On the evening of the day when Julie and her new friends took their collective bath, my phone rang. At the time I was looking at a collection of spurs that someone had brought to my office at my invitation. It is difficult, finding an agent one can rely on.

I was in the little office in one of my warehouses in Calgary. I like to answer the phone myself. I keep four offices, all with the same phone number. The person making the call was the elusive Billy Dorfendorf himself.

"Dorf here," he said. Just like that. Nothing more, nothing less. As if he had been away for a couple of hours and was possibly a few minutes late in returning a call I had made.

Dorf gave me the impression that he was in a great hurry. "Water under the bridge," he said, falling back on an unfortunate cliché. He made no mention of recent developments in our shared lives. "Water under the bridge," he kept saying. He declined to tell me where he was calling from, though Maggie in due course got the bill. He began to rave, while I wondered how I might quickly trace the call, about a collection of icons that was coming onto the market in a matter of days. He had just recently got wind of it, he said. The prize I had been seeking all my life, he said. This with not the slightest acknowledgement that I once paid him good money to find the perfect spa, and that with dire consequences.

I have always had a soft spot in my heart for the incredible colours and the refusal of perspective in those often anonymous paintings. Consider *St Theodose the Cenobiarch and an Unidentified Saint*; the two figures with their scarred eyes, creator unknown. Perhaps it is the anonymity of those who painted the icons that speaks most clearly to my concern, against the will of some to mark forever their work with their personalities. And with their prices. Anonymity too is a version of art.

We dickered. It became apparent that Dorf, short of cash as he invariably was and in a hurry to lay his hands on what he could never hold, was willing to enter into a difficult bargain. He had to get to the Greek island of Siphnos. With a stopover in Rome. He made no bones about what he was up to. That impractical man knew the cost to the penny.

"The icons are in Rome?" I asked.

"On Siphnos," he said, impatiently. "Siphnos. In the Cyclades. Some airhead professor has got hold of a large collection. We've got to deal fast."

I made him an offer. He said the advance I offered wouldn't even cover his expenses.

"It's the best I can do," I said. "Cut out your stop in Rome."

"I have to stop in Rome. Old friends."

Billy Billy Dorfendorf was the sort of man who went out of his way to avoid his friends. That was when I became suspicious.

The deal, I insisted, pretending that I might change my mind, would all have to be on the hush-hush. When collectors learned that I was in on the bidding, prices tended to shoot up.

Dorf and I talked for a long time. I was stalling, trying to guess what his motive might be. Obviously, he needed money and needed it badly. But his haste was untoward. Hurrying was one of the many things he didn't know how to do. Perhaps he was working with another collector somewhere in Rome. We chatted about Greece. I tried to make mention of my deceased wife, but he changed the subject back to icons. I was even reckless enough to make mention of Dr Manuel De Medeiros. "I sometimes think you did me a favour," I said. "That Portuguese doctor — what was his name? —"

"One of the icons," Dorf said, "is a representation of the face of God."

He was playing his trump card. The very notion intrigued me. It might, after all, be interesting to make a bid on the face of God. Dorf had guessed that I might be interested. Curiosity, you might say, killed the cat.

He had made some expensive calls to friends on Mount Athos, using Maggie's phone. It turned out that a number of icons had disappeared from one of the more isolated and more neglected monasteries. Fifteen altogether. The police were conducting an investigation — on Mount Athos.

"They'd have to be kept out of sight," Dorf suggested. "You couldn't go showing them in art galleries."

I countered with a little chariness of my own. "You'd have to act fairly quickly, Dorf. I can assure you that once they are in my possession —"

"Right," Dorf said. "Mum is the word. Jump is the command."

"Why so much emphasis on this one icon?" I was fishing and delaying at the same time, trying to get a glimpse into the workings of his treacherous mind. It wasn't that I was afraid of him. In a curious way, he was incapable of hurting a fly. "Is there only one decent icon in the lot? I would hope the other icons are of comparable quality."

"Major pieces. Major pieces." Dorf took a deep breath before he went on. "That one particular icon — the artist, apparently, saw him as — female. Saw her as female. God. The monks of Mount Athos — You know. Out of the public eye, if possible — Scandalous."

There was no way, really, I could avoid an entry into the bidding. I had never failed, I might add, to get a collection I decided I wanted to purchase. There are those who say, falsely, that I have on occasion stooped to means that border on the questionable.

The long and short of it was that Dorf and I talked a bit more but could not come to terms. He wanted complete freedom to negotiate as he saw fit, because, he said, of the parties involved. In a purchase of such importance — and I was beginning to conceive it as the commanding centre of my collection of collections, the completion of my enterprise — I wanted to have a hand in the matter. We agreed, in a civil fashion, to let the matter rest for a few days, then to talk again.

I could explain only too easily why Julie Magnuson and her friend were out of hiding, and I can assure you it had nothing to do with the wedding dress that I one day rather precipitously returned to the seamstress. I had a score, that day, to settle with both Julie and Fish, and I settled it. I am an up-front person. Dorf, when he phoned, neglected to tell me that Manny De Medeiros and my presumably deceased wife had waited out their time and had recognized an opportunity to lead me once more into a minefield of deceit and manipulation. Julie Magnuson could no longer stand not being the centre of attention.

We didn't exactly have a honeymoon, Julie and I. On the day after our wedding ceremony we went into the oil patch in northern Alberta. She had been teaching school in a town called Jackass Mountain. She didn't show up for work. I didn't show up to collect for the dress I'd returned to Josie Pavich. We didn't go to the church hall to open the gifts that had been intended for Julie Magnuson and her careless engineer.

We were out in the bush, Julie and I and a partner of mine, leasing oil rights in an area that was going to be swarming with crews and rigs the day the muskeg froze hard enough to carry heavy equipment. We were out in the bush in a cabin, the three of us together alone, for a whole summer and then into the fall too, and everything on our radio told us we were getting richer by the hour.

An accident occurred. Our partner was injured by a falling beam that left him stretched out on the floor with a broken back. Julie and I took a canoe and started out to get help, damn the ice and the portages. And we made it.

When the ice formed finally, and we got back to the cabin, Julie and I, with a couple of policemen and a bush plane, we were in for a nasty surprise.

We had left our partner with plenty of food and barrels of water. We hadn't guessed that a family of lynxes would get into the cabin. And then decide not to leave.

I tell you this only because, the bush plane and the two RCMP officers and the licked-clean bones gone over the horizon, Julie Magnuson announced that she preferred two men to one. She had liked, she said, the way we found ourselves living, there in that isolated place. She was not ashamed to be explicit. One man no longer satisfied her, she claimed. And I won't pretend that I didn't miss our friend too. He had built a sauna — it was a beam falling in the gloom of the sauna that injured him. He claimed he built it so Maggie could take a decent bath. But the three of us took to sitting in there together, not a stitch on, sweating like demons, flogging ourselves with birch boughs, laughing at all the mosquitoes and blackflies that wouldn't come near the steam and the smoke.

It was a far cry from that cabin to three classy homes. Julie and her doctor had elected to hide out in Italy and Portugal, if having the attention of secret, adoring patients can be called hiding out. For some reason many people who imagined themselves ill liked the special attention of a doctor who might one day abruptly make an appearance — then, the next day or that afternoon — and just as abruptly vanish. The guesswork itself became part of the cure, along with the soaking in tubs and pools, the drinking of gallons of water that wasn't fit to drink. They managed, and easily, to support three homes, Manny and Julie. One was in the village of Collodi, just a hop, skip, and a jump from the spa in Montecatini. It was a house that had something to do with Carlo Lorenzini and his creation of Pinocchio. Julie was inordinately proud of the connection. She invited Maggie to one day come see that place where the creator's name was lost while his puppet went on to a kind of immortal existence.

The second home was a villa on the edge of a forest on the outskirts of Luso, in Portugal, where Julie and Manny met. Freebooting Portuguese, calling themselves explorers, had collected together a forest of trees from the lands they had tried to collect as well. Julie

Magnuson had the gall to say I paid for that villa with the bribe I offered her doctor, which is nonsense; the services of even an incompetent spa doctor come high, yet are thought of as legal.

The third was an elegant home on a hidden street in Rome, somewhere between Via Flaminia and Viale del Vignola. It was close to and yet far enough away from Tivoli. It was from the last of these homes that Julie had departed on the morning of her startling appearance; it was to that house she retired after her splash in the Tivoli waters.

Her three homes, she explained to Maggie while they chatted over a bottle of grappa — an affectation of Manny's, intended as a sign of his virility — were each of them crammed to the rafters with every kind of figurine that ever was dug from the ground or lifted from under water. "You name it." She gestured around at the cluttered shelves, there in her parlour.

Julie Magnuson still, obviously, considered herself a collector who might make claims to being in my league. She showed no understanding at all of the difference between passion and will.

They chatted. Julie had a lot of talking to do; Maggie had a flight to wait for and was happy to listen. She heard about Manny's career and his work at Montecatini, the greatest of the Italian spas. And God knows the Italians should know about spas. Remember the Romans with their schemes and conquests and murders, all of them hatched in pools of warm water. But to hear Julie tell it, her miniature doctor was a regular little saint, helping the sick and the terminally ill when no one else would touch them, often taking no pay for his work.

What they said about the wedding dress, those two women, I have no idea. But surely they had a lot to say, and Julie, to Maggie's surprise, instead of so much as asking to see the dress, suggested that Maggie take it with her to her Greek island.

Maggie was ready to give it up then and there.

"Keep it," Julie insisted.

16

Josie Pavich and Ida Babcock, when they flew back to Vancouver, were not yet unpacked when they called Deadman Spring and asked for Fish. He, of course, was not at Deadman Spring at all; he was sitting among the headless torsos of various dress forms in Josie's living room, listening with both ears. They had hatched a little plot of their own, Fish and Ida and Josie, while flying across the Atlantic and drinking free booze.

Karen Strike answered the phone. In reply to Josie's questions she explained that Fish had not yet arrived back from his travels. Josie gave a cry of disappointment. Karen showed great concern and asked if something in their travel plans had gone awry.

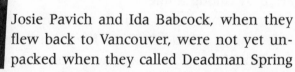

Josie Pavich, little vixen that she was, let Karen think she was persuading two helpless old ladies to spill the beans. Dear innocent Josie, with voice-over from Ida Babcock, said all there was to say about Henry Ketch's acquisition of the finest collection of icons to come on the market since the Swedes accepted a collection from the Russian revolutionaries in lieu of rubles — she said all that and more, and not a single word about Manny De Medeiros and Julie Magnuson. Nothing. Not one miserable word.

By the time Fish stopped gloating and said goodbye to his fellow conspirators, another day had slipped out of sight. He got back to Deadman Spring and found that Karen was gone. He learned from a note placed under a stone on his desk that Karen and her employer were off to a Greek island. As usual, Fish reacted by calling Rome.

Karen Strike and I arrived on Siphnos two days before Maggie sailed in on the ferry. We hired a helicopter that lifted us in from the Athens airport through a dazzling morning sky. There it was below us in the blue Aegean, the whole island, visible and complete. A perfect island, irresistible as a dream.

Karen travelled at my side because I have a bit of trouble with my eyes. Our pilot found a clear space on the beach at the little port of Kamares; he touched down just across the bay from the ferry landing. Karen and I hired a cab and headed up the impossible roads and around the hairpin corners toward the village that calls itself the capital.

Apollonia was too busy for my taste. Karen, in a matter of two hours, located a large house we could rent, in the village of Artemona, just above Apollonia. The agency called it a villa; I call it a mansion. But I found myself settling in before Karen had so much as completed the paperwork; before the sun had set I was rejoicing in the abundant light, the heat, the fig trees, the shade of a large pine, the taste of fresh bread and varieties of cheese and the local retsina.

It took Karen less than half the next day to track down Henry Ketch. Finding a nervous, anxious, fidgety art professor on a Greek island was about as difficult as finding the nose on your face.

Henry Ketch was a short and surprisingly wide man, with the blunted, glazed look of someone who thinks he has lost his glasses and is wearing them on his nose. He was, as his sons would on occasion tell him, losing it. For all his joviality, he was at his wit's end. He was counting on his wife once again to save him.

His two Greek partners had given him a choice of the islands he might use to stage his illegal removal of icons from Greece. He chose Siphnos because it was an island among numerous islands. It had on it a confusing number of chapels and in them a confusing number of icons. The coastline of the small island was dotted with small harbours, deserted beaches, hidden inlets and bays.

Henry fancied himself attractive to fellow creatures. Karen guessed as much the moment she saw the flourish with which he poured himself a glass of wine. He was having an early dinner all by himself at an outdoor restaurant in Apollonia.

"You look like someone who speaks English," she said. "May I sit down?"

She both hesitated and smiled.

He motioned her into the empty chair at his small table and with a magnanimous gesture signalled the waiter to bring another wineglass.

That they talked goes without saying. Henry Ketch needed a listening ear and welcomed, as we so often do, the combined ignorance and sympathy of a stranger. Karen explained all her cameras, when she could get in a few words, by saying she worked for a collector who would collect anything that could be loaded into the hold of a boat.

"Is that so?" Henry said. "Is that so?"

Karen Strike could bargain the hide off an alligator and then send the poor creature back into the pond. "I'm not supposed to talk about him," Karen said. She glanced at Henry's plate. "That calamari looks irresistible."

"It's smack on," Henry agreed.

"Do you mind if I order a little snack?" She lifted his wine bottle out of its melted ice and its olive oil can. "Should we have another?"

Julie Magnuson and one of her chauffeurs delivered Maggie Wilder to the airport in Rome; Maggie caught her flight, then stayed a night in Athens, then next morning took a cab to the dock in Piraeus and boarded the ferry to Siphnos.

The trip was nearly seven hours long. When the ferry landed in Kamares, Henry Ketch was there in the inevitable crowd that gathers to watch a ferry arrive, and at first Maggie didn't see him. Or perhaps she didn't recognize him. He was wearing shorts striped in gold and red, a pink T-shirt, a floppy purple hat. Henry was into power colours and believed he knew what they were. He was wearing sandals and a grin and carrying a woven shoulder bag of a sort popular among tourists on small islands. He imagined himself some kind of winner on no end of counts.

He seized Maggie's two bags as if she had suddenly become helpless and led the way off the pier and down along the promenade to a string of restaurants and cafés directly on the water's edge. Their rooms, he explained, after the usual exchange of pleasantries, were in a small private home inland in the village of Apollonia.

"Can we walk?"

"It's an hour walk uphill. It's a ten-minute ride on the bus — if you don't mind sitting on the lap of someone who is sitting on someone's lap who is sitting on someone's lap."

"You mean it's crowded."

"Precisely."

"Let's try it."

"Hang on, relax." Henry put down her bags beside a table. "A friend of yours is taking us for a ride. Around the island on a boat."

"I've been on a boat for seven hours, Henry."

"She says she knows you," Henry said.

"I don't know a soul on this island. I'm not sure I know you. Or want to."

"You're exhausted, Maggie, I can see it in your face." Henry explained excitedly that he had been approached the evening before, while eating calamari and drinking a bottle of retsina, by an elegant and shamelessly forward woman who was carrying enough cameras and equipment to weigh down a donkey. "Karen something."

"Strike," Maggie said.

"That's it!" Henry retrieved and set down again the bag that Maggie tried to pick up. "Right on. You know her. She says she saw you at Dead — Deadhead something."

"She saw me. I didn't have on any clothes."

Henry was ordering coffee. He had been on the island for eight days. "Quietly going mad," he explained. "I've quietly been going stark raving mad."

"So what's new?" Maggie said.

Henry was talking. He and his two associates had delivered the icons to the island. Or at least, the two associates had delivered the icons. They owned a small boat. They had gone back to Thessaloniki. Henry was in charge now. The coffee came and he explained again. The island was perfect for hiding icons. But he was uneasy. His two associates didn't want to take their boat out of Greek waters; the last leg of the journey was up to Henry.

"I don't get it," Maggie said. "Why all the secrecy?"

"I've been trying to explain, Maggie. You aren't listening." Henry, waving his right arm, spilled coffee into the lap of his gold and red shorts. "There are four hundred and twenty-four chapels on this island. This beautiful damned island is mapped by chapels as the night sky might be said to be mapped by stars." He paused to let her appreciate his rhetoric. He tried to brush the spilled coffee off his shorts. "The icons are stacked away in one of those chapels. So the next move is mine."

"So this afternoon you're going to show them to Karen Strike."

"Not on your sweet life."

Maggie paid and they got up from the table. Henry would say no more; his feelings were hurt. They tried shopping for pottery and Maggie found a vase she liked. Henry couldn't resist then: he explained to her that she couldn't possibly carry it with her. Back to Vancouver he added, and waited, hoping to learn what her plans were. If he couldn't tell her how to transport one clay pot, Maggie responded, how was he going to get fifteen icons out of Greece and then, on top of that, sell ten of them for his partners?

Henry checked for a coffee stain on his shorts.

"Looks like you wet yourself," Maggie said. "Did you wet yourself?"

"You saw me spill the coffee, Maggie. You aren't listening."

"I've done nothing but listen since I got here and all I've determined so far is that you're headed directly for another one of your exquisite disasters."

"Okay, so I haven't quite got things worked out."

They wandered aimlessly back to the table they had just a few minutes earlier left. They sat down again. The waiter ignored them.

"You said five minutes ago that you had."

"Had what?"

"Nothing, Henry."

"I said I might have things worked out. This Karen woman. She's the key."

"I'm trying to tell you, Henry. She'll have you for breakfast."

"You just watch me. If I can acquire fifteen icons from under the noses of patriarchs and patrol boats, I can get them off this island."

Maggie groaned. Then she braced herself to ask the question she had resolved while on the ferry not to ask. It was none of her business. Let him stew in his own juice, he liked it that way.

"There's something I have to know."

"Fire away."

"Are they stolen, Henry? The icons."

Henry bit at the left side of his lower lip.

"You're biting your lip, Henry. That's always a bad sign with you."

"Well. Okay. Yes. Let's say we didn't have permission to remove them from the old monastery where they were stored and starting to rot. I'm allowing myself one indiscretion in my long life. After all this — straight as an arrow. The straight and narrow."

"Your short life as a criminal."

"Exactly, Maggie. I've worked on this for years. For years. Now I have a collection, right here on this island, in a deserted chapel. Fifteen icons. How am I going to get them off the island and then sell two-thirds of the loot? That's the only question that remains."

"I say send them back to Mount Athos."

"Maggie, listen. Get this. If I bring this off I can sit in my study for the rest of my life and look at the real thing. I'm sick of looking at bad colour slides and trying to remember what I saw in a badly lit chapel. The real thing. I'll have it — there in my study. I'll never have to stay in another ratty hotel." He stopped. "Right now I don't know whether to shit or go blind."

"I say send them back to Mount Athos. And maybe you should go with them. Become a monk."

Maggie hated the costume Henry was wearing. Papa B, making a shadow puppet, would dress him in a dunce cap and sunglasses and give him a rattle to shake. She realized she had picked up the impulse from Papa B. She wanted to make up a story, try it, act it out, make changes if the ending didn't suit her.

The boat was coming straight at them. The man at the wheel cut the inboard motor. The silence made Henry look up at the boat that Maggie was watching.

The open boat was large enough to carry a dozen passengers. At first Maggie thought the three people seated in the stern were simply coming in to pick up customers for the day trip to one of the small, isolated beaches not too far distant along the island's rocky shore. Then she remembered it was afternoon.

"Look." Henry was pointing. He glanced at his wristwatch. "Right on the button."

The woman in the approaching boat was waving, trying to get their attention.

The man at the wheel brought the boat up to the promenade. But neither sailor made an effort to tie up.

One of them moved forward and caught hold of an iron ring set into the cement of the promenade.

"You can't go with them," Maggie said. "Henry. Listen."

Henry started to make introductions.

Karen made no gesture of recognition. "We have," she said, "tons of food and wine."

Maggie picked up the bag that held the wedding dress. Henry picked up her second bag; she took it from him and turned away.

She caught a bus that took her up the tortuous road to the village of Apollonia. Her heart lifted along with the bus. The whitewashed buildings of the village gave their startling light to the terraced hillsides. The bus moved into the village, then to the village square. She retrieved her two bags when they were tossed down from the roof of the bus; she looked again at the map Henry had scrawled on the back of an envelope.

Damn, she told herself. Just my luck. I like it. Sunshine and bougainvilleas. The pleasant, rich smell of donkey manure in the loud streets instead of rain and solitude. The elbowing rub of people busy with being daily and alive.

She took her own good time, looking for the private home where Henry had taken rooms. She walked away from the small square in the middle of the village; she returned and walked in another direction; she found, as Henry had said she would, a grape arbour set into a wall. She entered the welcome shade and reached through a doorway to knock at an open door.

Before Maggie could decide how to explain who she was, an old woman wearing a heavy black dress took the two bags and led the way through a kitchen, into a hallway beyond. Before Maggie's eyes could adjust, she was alone in a bedroom that opened onto a tiny second room that had in it a chair, a table.

She had got too much sun on the decks of the ferry; now she wanted to rest. But first she opened a bag, hung up a skirt and a blouse, draped a pair of shorts over the chair that was pushed against the small writing table. The rooms smelled of fresh flowers that were nowhere to be seen.

Trying to rest on the deep, sagging bed, she found herself worrying about Henry. She lay immobile, half asleep, half awake, wanting him to return at once and never to return from his boat ride, worrying at the same time about his prolific incompetence. With her luck she would end up hiding him, a fugitive, in these two rooms.

Night fell. Henry had not returned. The Siphnos night was full of stars. And, Maggie told herself, full of jagged coastline and submerged rocks, full of dark, twisting, cliff-bordered roads that inspire bus drivers to feats of daring.

She had worried like that a hundred nights, a thousand nights. She had sat alone in a small room she was sharing with Henry, sometimes with two small sons as well. She had learned techniques for waiting: delay reading the end of a book, walk the long way round to a shop, postpone a purchase — while Henry went first to a chapel, then to a taverna to make notes in the solitude he claimed he must have. Instead of being angry, she had listened for the sound of his return. And one night, in the silence, she began to write a story. And then another. And then the stories began to tell her what to do with her own precious life.

She heard the taxi over the faint sound of disco music. She was irked and relieved to see Henry in the doorway and alive. The landlady had left for him bread and olives and ouzo and a dish of baked chick-peas on the kitchen table. Maggie poured him a glass of ouzo and added the dash of water that turned it milky.

"Had to stop and see my mule drivers." Henry was anxious, exhausted, elated all at once. "Told them what to do in the morning. Gave them their instructions."

Maggie moved the food to where he sat down at the kitchen table. She refused to ask him the questions he wanted her to ask.

"One million," he said. "One million flat. No questions. No tax."

"You showed Karen Strike the collection of icons?"

"No way, Maggie. I just made the deal."

"She bought a pig in a poke? For one million dollars? And then you woke up."

"It's all arranged, Maggie. It's all set."

"I'll bet everything is all set. They're going to rob you and kill you. And then they'll dump your corpse in the sea for the octopuses."

"Octopi." Henry hesitated over the piece of octopus he was about to eat, then dipped it into a mixture of olive oil and sage and oregano and popped it into his mouth. "Safe as a church." He laughed wickedly at his joke. "I'm not going with the mule drivers. They know where the chapel is. They're getting paid enough money. Let them take the chances."

He was talking aloud but speaking to himself, rehearsing the plan. "Crack of dawn." He emptied his glass of ouzo and coughed. "The mule skinners move the icons out of the mountains."

He watched while Maggie poured his glass full again.

"Down to a harbour." He pointed across the table as if she must know what he meant. "Just down from here, on the coast. There's a hidden harbour."

Maggie joined him at the table. She read to herself the number that was the name on the ouzo bottle: Dodeka.

"The village of Kastro — up on a high rock. An acropolis. . . . A beautiful village. And right below the village there's a tiny harbour. You'd have to fall into it to find it."

"And you're going to find it, Henry? Or fall into it?"

Henry, wearily, excitedly, sipped his ouzo, broke another chunk of bread from the small loaf. "Why aren't you shouting with joy?"

"Okay. I'm shouting."

"We're rich. We can do whatever we like."

"You're rich. Leave me out of this. I have nothing to do with it."

"There's a chapel between Kastro and the harbour. It's up on a cliff, just below the village, straight above the harbour."

Maggie tried again. "Show me one hundred drachmas."

"That's where I meet Jack Deemer. Karen delivers Jack Deemer to that chapel. My mule skinners deliver the icons to the chapel. I'm on the boat that's waiting in the harbour. Karen shows up at the edge of the cliff and gives a wave. There's a path from the foot of the cliff. I climb up to the chapel."

"And then Jack Deemer writes you a personal cheque and takes the collection."

"Jesus, Maggie. Listen. He takes a look at the icons. First of all he has to approve, he has to want them. But he won't be able to resist. I know that. Then he gives me one million bucks in new American bills. One million. I count my money. Then the icons are his."

"And what do you do with your share of the icons? Carry them out through Customs on your back?"

Henry said nothing.

"You aren't answering."

Henry, biting into his bread, bit his thumb. "Damn. . . . He wants all of them, Maggie."

" — — — "

"This guy Deemer. Karen says he wants the whole collection or nothing. That's how he works."

"Henry. You were going to have them in your study. Your share. You have that book to write . . . "

"Shit." Henry's arms collapsed onto the table.

Maggie wanted blindly to reach across the table and reassure him. She was for a moment tempted to join him in his one and only crime, then tell him how to do it right.

"You haven't tried the chick-peas," she said.

"I've been eating chick-peas for eight days. Waiting here. Waiting for you. Trying to . . . decide."

"Maybe when you actually meet Jack Deemer —" Maggie heard the futility of her suggestion and stopped.

"Things didn't work out." Henry bit at his lower lip. He tried to lift his voice into optimism. "But once I get the money I can become a collector on my own. I can scour the world for icons. I'll offer cash on the barrelhead."

"Henry?"

He didn't want her to speak. He started to tell her how he would take a cab, just before dawn, down to Faros, a harbour south along the coast from Kastro. A luxury boat, there, waiting. He'd head out — look like a tourist. He'd be perfectly safe. Point the way to Kastro. Couldn't tell the captain until they were out at sea. Deemer was paying for the boat, a big fast thing —

"I brought my wedding dress with me," Maggie said.

She was telling Henry something. She was trying to tell him, things work out, don't panic. So it takes time.

Henry looked up sharply from his plate. "Am I losing my hearing?"

"You heard me."

"Planning to get married?" Henry tried to stab an olive with a fork. "Maggie, we have work to do."

"It still fits, you know. How about that?"

"Your boobs must have grown."

"Henry, you're a disaster. But not a hopeless disaster."

"It didn't quite fit. Don't you remember? You had to stuff the boob part with wads of toilet paper."

"Henry, I'm trying to talk."

"Well say something."

She couldn't think of what it was she wanted to say.

"Jesus H," he said. "My whole life is on the line, I'm breaking the law, risking my career, trying to land the big one. And you talk about a wedding dress. Listen. It made you look like a doll. Okay? Some kind of great big toy doll."

"How do you know? You didn't look at it when I had it on. You were too busy fretting because you thought I was pregnant."

"Hey. Listen. I told you then I didn't like the dress, don't sit there looking surprised."

"You did not tell me you didn't like it."

"Okay, I hated that dress then, I hate it now. It's gawdy and awful. Pictures, for God's sake, on a wedding dress. Two-headed magpies. Sky-blue mountain goats. A pickaxe. A rainstorm. Half the main street of some town that's dead and gone. I wanted you to wear a straight street-style suit, a small bouquet of something or other, nothing fancy. And you *were* pregnant, it turned out."

"I wanted to get married because I found that wedding dress, Henry, not because we thought I might be pregnant. Accept it. Live with it."

"I know, Maggie, I read your goddamned story. You got married to a wedding dress, not to me. Don't tell me about it."

"That story was not about us."

"So who the hell was it about? You knew that dress was a second-hand, hand-me-down streak of bad luck looking for somewhere to happen. It was a bad luck dress, so why couldn't you leave it alone? Why couldn't you keep your hands off it? Don't answer. I'll tell you. That dress is the disaster, not me. Send it back to where it came from."

"Fuck you, Henry Ketch. Let's just get your criminal activity over with so I can catch a flight and go back to Vancouver. I'm still stupid enough to try and keep you out of jail."

"Fine," Henry said. "Fine. Tomorrow morning is the beginning of the first day of my life and all that shit, so give me a break. Take the first ferry out to anywhere. Or back to nowhere."

Maggie stood up and left the kitchen.

She went into their bedroom and unpacked the dress she hadn't been able to unpack. She spread the wedding dress over her left arm and went out through the kitchen and past Henry, through the grape arbour and into the dark street. She followed the street into the village square, then decided she must leave that too. The lights and the sound of music behind her, she chose a street at random and entered it.

Ten minutes later she was alone in front of a chapel. She entered the chapel.

Inside, candles burned, giving a faint light to the icons on the altar screen. The icons were numerous, crowded together, badly lit by flickering candles, some high on the screen, some almost touching the inlaid marble floor. The walls beside and behind her were covered with icons as well. A model of a ship hung from the ornate ceiling, a gift, no doubt, of sailors who had returned gratefully from the sea. Maggie closed the door and was surrounded. Her turning to look at the surrounding walls made the flames on the little forest of candles flicker and leap. She was enclosed, immersed; the icons flared gold; the gold flared into the stillness of brown, into the thrust of red. The colours took form; colours turned into cloaks and cowls; clothed bodies erupted into the nakedness of face.

It was a chapel built from the stones and over the stones of a temple to Artemis. There, that night, innocent, not knowing, she saw among the faces a face that whispered her a message. Or, turning, and turning again, she did not see but rather realized she had seen a face among those sainted faces; she had seen one different face, behind the filigree of silver, behind a clouded glass. She knew the lips of the face had moved.

The silence made her dizzy. She groped for the door that had lost itself among the many icons.

She began to climb the winding, narrow stone street. The street was a series of long, sloping steps. Two young people came down the steps toward her. Seeing Maggie, they veered away from each other, and were about to pass her, one on either side. Maggie dared to greet them in English. The young woman replied with a tentative hello?

"Artemona," Maggie said. She gestured with her raised hands, making the word a question.

The young man nodded and with one forefinger pointed downward, drew a wide circle around Maggie's head. She had left the village of Apollonia. She was in the village of Artemona.

Maggie then tried to ask where she might find a large house, and in the large house a foreigner. "*Canadezos*," she said. She waited. "*Geros*," she added. She took a few steps, walking as if tottering. She had never seen Jack Deemer, and yet she must describe him. "And with the man," she tried to explain, "a woman with cameras." She raised her hands in front of her right eye and pretended to take a picture.

The young woman giggled and went and stood beside the young man, pretending to be photographed. Then the young woman pointed at the dress that Maggie carried on her left arm.

Maggie shook her head. "No. Oh, no. I am not getting married."

"Yes," the young woman said, risking a word in English, smiling at the young man. She pointed then up at the night sky. She was, apparently, indicating a time or a season. Maggie, looking up, saw only the Big Dipper.

She was lost again. Or at least she could not find the house she sought. There were a number of large houses along the narrow street. She was stepping around a pair of old women seated on chairs almost in the middle of the street, outside a brightly lit doorway, when both old women cried out at once, "Oh, *Panagiamou*."

They were pointing at the dress on Maggie's arm.

Maggie stopped and held up the dress to their gaze. But that was not enough to satisfy them. They insisted that she hold the dress against her body. The two women nodded approvingly, speaking rapidly in Greek. They touched the dress. Then Maggie in turn insisted on holding the dress against each of the two small women and their black dresses and shawls.

They were laughing, obviously making jokes along with offering praise; the dress concealed them each in turn; they would not themselves try to hold the dress. They together shook their heads. They couldn't possibly touch it.

Then Maggie, once again holding an imaginary camera, indicated that she needed directions. The two women did not understand. Maggie, over and over, mimed her need. She tried to pretend that she was carrying a burden of cameras. She mimed the taking of photographs of the two old women, but to no avail. She mimed being lame and blind and bald. She raised in front of herself the wedding dress as if she might be posing to be photographed with the man she had mimed. "Old," she said. "*Geros.*"

"Oh, *Panagia-mou,*" they cried at once, the two old women. Miming now in turn, talking all the while, waving their hands and pointing and motioning Maggie to try and keep up in the faint light, they led the way.

They walked in the Siphnian night, high above the sounds of disco music that came up from the streets below. They turned away from the bed of a dry stream and climbed again, up a series of long stone steps, and turned again, into a cobbled street that was bordered on either side by stone walls.

The two old women would go no farther. They pointed and spoke excitedly in Greek. One of the old women raised her hands in front of her face and pretended to take a picture. The other woman dropped her shawl off her grey hair and pointed at her hair and nodded vigorously.

Maggie went on by herself. There was only one gate at the end of the narrow street.

She had found Jack Deemer's rented house. It was a splendid house, almost a villa, a magnificent house built of stone and stucco into the slope of a terraced hillside. The first floor of the house opened off the cobbled street. The wall of the house might simply have been the wall of the terraced hillside, except that an iron gate opened in on a stairway. Maggie peered in through the gate. Inside was a stone stairway. To the right of the stairway a heavy wooden door opened into the lower floor of the house. The stone stairway itself, open to the night, seemed pointed at that sky.

Maggie reached through the iron gate and unhooked it and let herself in. Slowly, cautiously, she went up the flight of stone steps.

She was on a large patio. To her right, a short flight of steps led to a still higher patio and a row of windows and doors. To her left was the main patio, with beyond it a garden, beyond the garden on three sides, walls.

Maggie saw in the garden, in the shadowy light, two fig trees, their leaves large, clotted together in shadow.

They marked the edge between the garden and the patio. There was a clothesline strung between the two large fig trees, the tops of three bikinis pinned to the line. Maggie needed the clothes pegs. She removed the bikini tops and dropped them onto a deck chair.

It was on that clothesline that she hung the wedding dress. It became, in the light from the night sky, a pale white scarecrow. She hung it carefully on the line, then brushed out the creases. It was impossible, in that light, to see the embroidery, the beadwork. In that bright and shadowy darkness, the dress was white.

Dress in a landscape, she thought. Good title. Must go write that down.

Perhaps she intended, should I prowl sleepless on my patio, or in my garden, to give me the fright of my life. Or the revelation.

I should say that I do not walk lame; my stride is vigorous and enduring. And I might add that I am not bald; my hair, however grey, falls in long and graceful waves to my shoulders. Maggie, in her ignorance, in her trespassing, could know none of this. All perhapses aside, it was surely her intention that I should, one way or another, encounter the ghost of Julie Magnuson.

17

Maggie and Henry sat down to breakfast at that time before dawn when the first light is more a trace in the mind than in the window or on the horizon.

Henry Ketch was wildly angry at himself for not demanding more money for the collection. Karen, acting for Deemer, had simply wondered if he'd settle for one million dollars flat, one million even, no questions asked, and Henry had almost nodded his head off before she finished speaking. "Goddamn," he was saying now, while he smashed the boiled egg he was trying to crack, "would you believe how stupid I am? Years. Fourteen years of scheming. I got this idea fourteen years ago, one time when we were staying in a place so small we had to back into the toilet."

"Henry, please." Maggie was enjoying herself. "You're overwrought."

She cut in half a slice of the hard, dry local cheese, manoura, and wished for margarine to go with the bread. "Hang in for two more hours. Once they load that boat you'll be loaded yourself. Unless they decide to slit your throat and drown you."

"Don't sound so hopeful."

He began again to recite the plans. He was to board a boat that was waiting in Faros. Faros, he explained, lighthouse, get it? She said she got it. She sampled the bread and cheese and tried the coffee. The boat would then sail, as if on a pleasure cruise, the few kilometres around the easternmost point of land to Saralia — the harbour below the high village of Kastro. It was a perfect, deep cleft of a harbour, almost totally concealed by cliffs. And on the cliff to the north of the harbour was the chapel where the transaction would take place. All Henry had to do was ride the boat into the harbour and then wait, sit still, stay out of danger, until he received a signal.

"Perfect," Maggie said. "What could possibly go wrong, besides everything?"

"And you, dear?" Henry was trying to put honey on a slice of bread with the back of a spoon. "Thyme. You can taste it." He touched the spoon to his lips. "Wonderful. I want you to share the booty."

"The booty. The loot. Another Crusader has arrived to save the island and is about to depart."

"You're getting into the spirit of things, Maggie."

"The Venetian merchants have sent one last trader to the silver mines of the island."

Henry banged approvingly on the table with the spoon; it stuck to the table.

"Henry, just lend me enough for a ferryboat ride. I'm low on cash. I'm going back to Athens on the first ferry."

"Sit tight, Maggie. Stick with me and you'll be wearing diamonds."

"Just lend me twenty bucks."

"We'll call in a helicopter, go out of here in style. We'll go home. We'll buy a new house."

"More space for you to hang your icons. And I'm not going with you — not anywhere — past the Athens airport."

"Stop it, Maggie. Patience. You've got to be patient. The butterfly comes to the collector who sits still."

"Spare me the message, Henry. Is that too much to ask from a learned man?"

And then he was angry at himself again. "Two million. Two million or nothing. Two million flat would be nothing to that thief, Jack Deemer. Chicken feed. Pocket money. Four of us in that boat. That Karen whatever. She wanted to know if the deal pleased me, if I was happy. Happy. That was her word. Happy. Was I happy? I was like a goddamned prisoner. What could I say?"

"Even now, you could say the deal's off."

"Maggie. Listen. I think you're deaf."

"Go meet your mule team and take the icons and run."

"Where would I run to, Maggie? How do you run — with icons painted on great huge slabs of wood that the devil himself couldn't lift?"

"You want the money, Henry. Face it."

Henry sipped his instant coffee. "I have to deliver the goods. Have to. One false move, Karen said, and I'm in the octopus garden. She said it like she was telling me to try the local honey." He tore open another roll and reached with his spoon and smeared honey inside the roll and dabbed the roll into his coffee.

"I can't stand it," Maggie said.

The old woman who had got up before dawn to provide them with breakfast came stooping into the kitchen. "Taxi," she said, stressing the second syllable. "Taxi. Taxi."

Henry, leaping up, knocked his caned chair backward onto the tiled floor. Maggie put her hands over her ears.

"Henry. Relax. You'll be there one hour early. There's no hurry."

"Come with me, Maggie." Henry elbowed aside the old woman and her weight of black clothing, then stopped in the doorway. "Please. This one last favour. Cross my heart and spit to die. Just come along as far as the boat."

"Stop the helpless child routine, Henry. And what would I do once you lured me onto the boat? Watch in the dark for an invisible harbour that you're supposed to know how to find?"

"Just come along. Like you're holding my hand." And then he added, incongruously, "I notice you've stopped smoking. Congratulations."

"I'm on my way," she said.

"Please."

Maggie heard herself relenting. "I should get our packing done, don't you think, Croesus? Get out of here."

She sat and finished her breakfast. The old woman tipped another spoonful of instant coffee into Maggie's cup and added a few drops of water, used the spoon to beat the coffee creamy in the bottom of the cup, then added hot water from a kettle she lifted from a hotplate. Maggie sipped the coffee and picked at the cheese and bread that Henry had left on his plate.

Dawn, against all her wishing, broke. She admitted to herself that she was about to delay her departure by one day. She borrowed a black sweater from the old woman. It would be at most a four-kilometre walk to Kastro. She learned that much, using her few words of Greek. By the time she arrived in Kastro, Henry's boat would be in the harbour under the village — assuming he and it didn't get lost.

Roosters crowed. Donkeys brayed. The first heat raised itself up under the cool of night. Maggie began to doubt her own purpose. She could go in the opposite direction, down the longer road to Kamares, and there sit on the beach, loaf away the day. She could return to the village of Apollonia after a leisurely lunch and watch while Henry tried to count to one million, and then she could listen while he complained about the high cost of calling in a helicopter and suggested that they take the ferry instead.

The column of mules, on the hillside across the valley, caught her attention but did not arouse her curiosity. The loaded animals might be carrying stone and lumber and cement and water to any site on any mountainside. She tried casually, to count the mules as they disappeared down the deep-worn trail, then reappeared from behind stone walls or out of olive groves. They seemed to move of their own accord. Then there appeared a peasant following after. Maggie guessed there must also be someone leading the mules. She watched the stone walls and the terraced fields, the groves of grey-green olive trees, the open fields with their sage and capers and thistles. She followed along on the crudely paved road that stayed to a ridge that paralleled the old mule trail. After a while she caught a glimpse of a man as old and ragged as his comrade, leading the mules. Or at least he led the first mule. The halter of the second mule was tied to the tail of the mule ahead of it, and so on, to the seventh mule in the column.

After a while she recognized that each mule was loaded with two large and awkward parcels, each parcel wrapped in blankets or sacking.

The morning sky was unnervingly clear.

The village of Kastro crowns a high outcrop of rock. If, just as dawn is breaking, you set out to walk the road from Apollonia down into the valley and then up onto the outcrop of rock, you can see, far distant, the Aegean coming alive with light.

It was a glistening dawn, the sea a violet blue. Maggie wanted to let herself weep with simple joy. Or perhaps she wanted to weep to relieve her tension. The far, stuccoed, whitewashed walls of the village were seemingly as old as the rocks that gave them their stilled, soaring grace.

In the near darkness of the valley below the paved road on which Maggie walked, the mules moved in a slow procession, sometimes invisible. Listening carefully, she heard behind the sound of roosters and donkeys the delicate clink of hooves on pebbles and stone.

It was a long time before she realized there was a third person in attendance. A monk was following along but stopping now and then, vanishing behind an abandoned stone house or an olive tree. It was apparent to Maggie that he was taking precautions to stay out of sight. Either he was a guard, watching out for the two mule drivers, or they were not aware they had company.

They were walking. It was dawn and they were all walking, the sun inviting them. They moved with the appearance of being in no hurry. Maggie was walking along a highway from which she could see below her a considerable valley where a long trail led down from the fields and the village of Apollonia and then through the valley, behind a low mountain, and up toward Kastro. The mules moved down the trail in their careful, deliberate, watchful way. Each mule was loaded with two large, awkward parcels that in their height exaggerated the motion of the mules.

They disappeared behind the low mountain, the mules and their drivers. Then Maggie could see only the monk's tall hat. He walked between two high stone walls, the steep trail paved with stone steps that gave back to him and to Maggie the sound of the hooves of the disappearing mules.

The highway took Maggie away from the mule trail, around the low mountain. She walked faster but not too fast, afraid she would lose the mule train, afraid she might, by hurrying, get ahead of it and the monk.

Moving around the mountain, she saw above her and to the left of the road, up on the mountainside, the remains of a stone windmill. Realizing that from there she could at once watch and remain out of sight, she stepped off the road and climbed through the thistles and weeds and capers toward the broken ruins that had been the round tower of a wind-driven mill.

As she approached the mill, the monk she had been watching stepped out of the doorless doorway; he stood, blatantly, watching her approach.

Maggie wavered. Then she decided she would not turn back. She would not be intimidated.

Maggie Wilder had never seen her Papa B at a distance. For all her acquaintance with his immediate presence, she had never had occasion to see the man in a landscape. He was a tall man made taller by his hat. If anything betrayed him, it was his walk. He seemed, even as he moved around the side of the mill, to be stealing away from something rather than toward.

Maggie began to hurry. She was gasping for breath as she hurried up the steep slope. She wanted to shout and couldn't. Papa B looked down into the valley on the far side of the mill, then he returned to the doorway.

He is always in a doorway, Maggie thought. There he is, for God's sake, where is his pizza delivery? She wanted then to shout at him. Calamari and olives. She was climbing the hill. Green tomato and eggplant and soujoukakya.

It was Dorf who spoke. Standing there in the doorway that was too low to allow for his hat, his head ducked outside the doorway, his body inside, he called in a desperate, suppressed voice, "Where is she?"

Maggie stumbled against the rough stone wall and stopped, gasping.

"She's not in Rome," he said. "I was there. She's here on the island. Where is she?"

He was all slicked up. He had washed his hair, the knot of hair at the back of his head was as tight as a small fist. He had trimmed and combed his beard. His clothes didn't smell of sweat and urine.

Maggie indicated that she was trying to catch her breath.

"Those icons." Dorf caught her by the hand. He led her away from the doorway, around the mill. Below them on the trail the mule train moved with a maddening slowness. "They'll lead us to her, won't they?"

He was still as batty as ever, however he might look. Maggie saw that.

He was pleading for her help. He was, in his strange way, begging her. But now it was she who needed the help. He might at least have asked; he might have wondered what the icons were doing to her as well as to him.

"Where's your husband?" Dorf asked.

"He's supposed to be on a boat in the harbour."

"To take him to safety, I hope."

Maggie rushed to Henry's defence. "For a change he's using his brains. Your friend Karen Strike is here to do the dirty work. Along with her boss."

Only then did Dorf realize that Jack Deemer was on the island.

Dorf betrayed nothing, behind his beard. "Where is he?"

"Henry? I told you —"

"Deemer. Jack Deemer. Where did you see him?"

"I haven't seen him."

"Then how do you know he's here?"

"Karen Strike. She told Henry. Henry told me."

Dorf took Maggie by the hand and started down the slope.

"Let me catch my breath, please."

"I have to talk to those mule drivers."

"Will Henry be okay?"

"If a stranger shows up on this island and hires seven mules —" Dorf was leading the way. They hurried down the slope, he and Maggie. They hurried past a second windmill, at the base of the acropolis. The back walls of the mediaeval houses formed a wall around the top of the high rock outcrop. Maggie and Dorf, where the highway ended against a heap of boulders, began to climb a steep path up toward that wall.

The early sun, hardly out of the sea, sprayed the whitewashed walls of the village a misty white. Dorf led Maggie into a dark passageway. Within the wall the air was cool and palpable. They found a stone stairway.

Inside the enclosing wall the whitewashed houses and their painted wooden doors faced onto a narrow street. Each flagstone in the street's surface was outlined in whitewash. Wooden stairways went up to arches and timbers that joined the second floors of facing houses.

"Up there," Dorf said.

He and Maggie climbed a stairway and found a landing where they could wait under a stone archway and watch the mules pass beneath. The sun was not yet high enough to light clearly the passageway below them. Dorf whispered as he explained: they will come straight through the village. If they go around, on that path along the cliff's edge, someone will get suspicious.

Maggie, answering, whispered in return. "I'm scared."

"Listen," Dorf said.

The sound of hooves on stone echoed distantly into the covered street. They could do nothing but wait, Maggie and Dorf.

Dorf whispered again. "Bludgett moved into your attic."

"He's still there?"

"Yeah."

"You mean — he moved into my attic?"

"He likes the puppets. He's learning to work with the puppets." Dorf listened again for the approaching mules. "I traded him the puppets for a ticket. He wouldn't lend me the fare, the bastard. Not a penny."

"Who looks after —" Maggie checked herself. Let him starve.

"Don't worry. He sends out for pizza." Dorf whispered against her ear. "Inez delivers it." He put a finger to his lips, then pointed down the covered way. "It turns her on. Going to see him there. Delivering the pizza. They wanted me out of the house. Inez told me to get out or she'd —" Dorf bumped his tall hat against the stone overhead; he caught the hat and, fumbling, put it back on.

"But —" Maggie said.

"She said she would make arrangements. A bottle of wine. A free pizza or two. Inez has connections."

It was not the mules that came into sight but rather Karen Strike. She came into the street from the opposite direction, moving toward the approaching mules; she was carrying a video camera and two camera cases and a black bag and a tripod.

"Balls," said Dorf.

The stone arch above brushed again at his tall hat; Maggie reached to catch it. He is, she thought, a monk after all. Being a fake monk is as close as he can get to being what he is.

The light came in from deep openings above them and turned to sagging patterns on the whitewashed walls. Maggie wanted the certainty of day.

Karen Strike needed light. Dorf held his breath as if to hold back the light itself. Karen found a stone stairway and went up a few steps to test the light. She stepped down again and retreated back the way she had come.

"Damned near gave me a heart attack," Dorf said.

Maggie liked him then. She remembered the way he had been, at times, in her attic.

The mules were there. They stopped in the walkway directly below Maggie and Dorf.

Maggie liked the smell of the mules. That was the first thing she noticed. She liked the ropes and knots and packstraps, intricate webs, that held the wrapped icons as upright as runes. She could not see anything of the icons and yet she understood Henry's fascination; she had tears in her eyes and everything she looked at was soft and blurred.

The two muleteers knew a small bar where they could get a quick drink of ouzo. They had been travelling for three hours. They left the mules and their loads standing in the narrow and covered street.

Dorf remembered just a little about handling mules. He had helped out on Mount Athos, while working as a logger in those months before he was put to work restoring manuscripts and icons.

"I need your help," he said to Maggie.

He had a plan. Billy Billy Dorfendorf always had a plan. There was a monastery on the sea's edge a few miles north of the village. He could, in a matter of minutes, direct the mules and their icons out of the village. The trail to the monastery was obscure. He had checked it out the day before while he was looking for Maggie. He had in his usual way gone to places where she was not likely to be; in the process he got wind of a famous professor who had hired a string of pack mules and ordered them kept in a state of readiness, as if the island expected one last swarm of pirates to show up on the horizon.

"Can you help?" he asked. "We might be doing Henry a favour."

Maggie remembered her attempts at helping Papa B in the attic in her house. He had a way of asking for help and then turning his helper into a mountain, a cliff. Or into a lover. She remembered that too and was tempted to reach across their hesitations and kiss him. She was tempted, one last time, to try to do Henry a favour.

"I want you to go and distract those two muleteers. Give me three minutes. Just tell them you want to have a drink. By the time they sort that out I'll be away."

Maggie's folly in agreeing had something to do with the guilt she felt at the sale of the icons. They were about to be loaded into a boat, then taken to Cyprus, then to one of the warehouses in Calgary, where Jack Deemer stored his collections. They would disappear. And then, Maggie thought, Karen Strike will return with her cameras and attempt to record what she helped make disappear.

"Let's hit it," Dorf said.

Maggie Wilder went to find the two muleteers and found herself instead on the balcony of a small café on the outside wall of the village of Kastro. She could look out over the sea but not down into the deep cleft of the harbour. There was no boat on the sea. Deemer's hired boat and Henry, she hoped, were arrived safe in port, whatever the plan. Little did she know that the invisible harbour had been a refuge to Phoenicians and Cretans, to the Venetians after them, in the long and necessary taking of booty. I, the collector, am their inheritor. Hadrian himself, hauling off the sculptures of Greece to his Roman gardens, did more than himself a favour.

Maggie didn't find the mule skinners. When she returned to tell Dorf of her failure she found him standing in a tangle of restless and snorting mules. And talking to Julie Magnuson.

Maggie Wilder knew Julie Magnuson in that suppressed light as Dorf would have known her in a pitch dark room. The air currents, the alterations in the shape of space itself, would have spoken to him her presence. He had once been her lover and after that his life had not ever known the security of solid ground.

Julie Magnuson and Dorf had embraced and had not been able to let go. What they said, if anything, to each other, Maggie Wilder could not hear, over the sounds of the mules and their packsaddles and their riggings and their hooves, and the knocking together of wrapped icons. Julie Magnuson was holding Dorf as if she had found one of the puppets that were the pride of his life.

Maggie turned and fled. The mules were in danger of running loose with their awkward loads. Maggie, in her need to make order of a chaos that she could only observe and regret, went once more to try and find the muleteers. What happened there in that covered street with Julie and Dorf together, the mules and the icons all around, is something I can at best speculate about.

And yet I am not without some knowledge. That they had been lovers together in Portugal was the commonest of knowledge, and that they, there in Kastro, embraced again, goes without saying. Julie Magnuson was always and rabidly the lover. She seized her men where she found them, and there in that multiplied, hidden, insidious street she found her William William Dorfendorf. What gropings they allowed against each others' bodies, I can only guess. Lust is merely lust; and yet it is lust. They went at each other, they seized each other. The frightened animals were not so close to abandon as were the reunited lovers. Julie was without qualm, and Dorf was always the first to respond in extreme and demeaning situations. That he could only respond was his nature, he was never the leader. He wanted again the humiliation he must have known when in bed together with Julie and her dwarf. The three of them had shamelessly made love. Manny was indeed not there at that moment, but he was, as it turned out, not far away. And Julie, what did she do? Did she tug and pull at Dorf's blue skirt? Did they fall in the dung that was everywhere at their feet? Maggie, to my embarrassment, insists she responds to the smell of the dung of donkeys and mules. And horses, she adds. Julie, too, thrilled to that animal world that offends me, that world of frank odours and acrid tastes and guttural sounds, that world without the decency of enduring shape. They, in their jagged, animal way, fucked, I suppose, Julie and Dorf. Or no doubt tried to. And no doubt failed.

When Maggie returned with the two muleteers who were by that time well into their cups and reluctant to get on with their job, Dorf was confused and alone.

"I won't let Jack Deemer have this," Dorf was muttering, to himself, to the mules. He was frantic. Spent. He was unable so much as to undo a simple square knot or double half-hitch, let alone a knot tied by a muleteer. Yet, all the while, he was trying to protect the tallest parcel from being bumped or damaged by the loads on the other mules. It must have stood a good eight feet in height to begin with, that tallest one. Mounted on a packsaddle, it was far out of reach of his fumbling hands.

Had he kept his wits about him he might have seen Karen Strike taking pictures in that impossible light. She had the courtesy, whatever else must be said of her, to send me copies of the pictures she took that difficult morning. What little she had managed to photograph of the two lovers was much interfered with by the movements of the frightened mules. Their bulky loads had further obscured the sight. And yet Karen, skilled photographer that she was, that she is, had got at least one photograph that suggested the truth of my speculations about the behaviour of the two lovers. In that one photograph Dorf is lying with his legs spread, his face turned to the right so that he is seen in profile. The head of a mule with its leather halter and its halter rope covers the space where his private parts must be, but it appears his skirt has been raised right up to his neck and beard. His arms are flung akimbo, in a gesture of surrender. Or ruin.

It was Karen's activities that restored the necessary order, given the drunken state of the two mule skinners. They had somewhere in a matter of minutes managed to get thoroughly pissed. The single eye of her camera, aimed at the confusion in the narrow street, made the muleteers and their mules alike fall into a straggly line. Little did she realize that in doing so she was directing them into the sights of Manny De Medeiros's rifle. It was time to leave behind the narrow and beautiful and, for all the confusion, safe street.

The two muleteers were dangerously drunk. They managed to squeeze their charges through a cleft between two abandoned stone houses, out onto the very track they had earlier been trying to avoid. But they had lost precious time. It would soon be too dangerous to move straight along the village's enclosed street. Already, a few citizens were stirring themselves awake, stepping out of small bedrooms to stretch and to yawn at the morning sun, to water a geranium growing in an olive oil tin, to walk through narrow alleys toward the bakery.

Maggie followed after the muleteer who followed after the last mule. Ahead of her, the ragged procession made its way along the treacherous cliffside path that clings to the slope just under Kastro's wall. From that path, stopped by her dizziness as she looked down toward the sea, she saw for the first time a shelf of bare rock jutting out into the sea, to its left a small grey chapel set squarely on a small mound of rock.

Maggie was certain Henry had made an error in his description. There was no cliff beside that chapel. Yet she believed she saw, far below, the place where he and Jack Deemer were to meet. There was no boat in sight. She panicked. No life stirred on the rockshelf or near the chapel. There were, at that early hour, three swimmers in the water, and all three hardly more than children: one girl and two boys, tourists, Maggie guessed, Germans or Swedes probably, and not willing to wait for the full of summer; they were visibly naked, even at that distance, swimming strongly in the blue, transparent water. Maggie leaned back against the hillside and fought to recover her balance. The sun was up. Something had gone wrong; everything had been delayed. One of the swimmers, the young girl, reached up and caught hold of a rock ledge, then lifted her tanned body out of the water and onto the ledge. She brushed water from her limbs, then, slowly, turning to face the two swimmers who on their backs let themselves float on the water, with extended arms appeared to lift the sun free of the water's hold, into the sky.

The caravan was nowhere to be seen. Maggie, coming to her senses, realized the mules had disappeared; on either side of the flinty path the patches of thistle and thyme caught at the sound of bees. Holding her breath and listening, Maggie heard somewhere ahead of her, over a rise, around a turn in the path, the reassuring sound of the hooves of the mules.

Everyone had vanished. Maggie followed after the faint sound that came now from below her, now off the stone wall to her right, now off the square cement houses farther ahead, built like the nests of swallows onto the wall's height.

She was balanced on the path's edge when she saw the chapel she was seeking. It was a small, sturdy chapel, a dazzling white in the morning sun, its barrel-vault roof parallel to her gaze, its nearest wall windowless. The mules were still not to be seen. Beyond the chapel was a deep cleft that must open down and become the harbour; beyond the farther rockface the open sea lifted itself against the curve of a blank horizon.

Maggie moved along the path to where she could see the small door that opened into the chapel on the landward side. Somewhere below her the mules had stopped making any sound.

As Maggie stopped to listen, a bride came out through the chapel door.

The two drunken muleteers came into view, leading their invisible mules. Then the mules were there too; the mule drivers brought their train to a halt.

Dorf and Julie and Karen, coming into view below Maggie, seeing the bride in the doorway, stopped in their tracks. No one had thought of the possibility of a wedding at that early hour.

Dorf was the first to move. He went on ahead by himself. He became the monk he had so long pretended to be, and now he was concerned, ready to offer apologies to the bride and her invisible groom — for the groom and the wedding party had, oddly, not yet emerged from the chapel. Dorf slipped past the mules and their loads.

Karen and Julie did not move, they only watched. Maggie Wilder, behind and above, watched them watching, then looked again to the solitary bride.

The rituals of love are many and various, and that of the wedding dress is stranger than most. The particular dress on that particular bride, of course, was not as white as it looked from a distance. Seen close up, it was a veritable mirage of colours and forms, a story of desire, of betrayal, of ragged lust, of barbarous fulfilment. The nimble fingers of Josie Pavich had scribbled on that cloth each tattle of gossip that came to her ignorant ears. She gave wings to a fish, one human eye to a wild rose bush. And yet, in the ticklish imaginings of her presumably virgin life, she overwhelmed.

I had first of all put on the dress simply as a disguise, to make sure no one would recognize me there at the chapel. I put it on. And then something precious happened.

Wearing the dress, I was no longer simply myself.

I cannot see well at all. I did not see the mules or their drivers or Julie or Maggie or Karen, there on the path above the chapel. All I saw was the looming ghost that was William William Dorfendorf, heir to two dead grandfathers who shared nothing but a given name.

My first impulse was to retreat into the chapel. I had been expecting Henry Ketch. Instead I was confronted by an old adversary, a man who had been one of my wife's lovers.

It was out of the goodness of my heart that I let him duck in behind me through the low green door of the chapel.

I had sat for nearly an hour in the chapel, after Karen left me there and went off to take photographs. The room was the size of a cell, four of my careful paces across, six in length. I found that out by pacing in the dark. After a while, as the sun became stronger, I saw where I might sit down. There were no pews in the room, only a bench along one wall, and facing it from the opposite wall a kind of double chair. I put down the red and blue canvas athlete's bag intended for Henry on one seat of the chair and sat beside it in the second; I watched the rays of the sun make their way in at the small, recessed window and down the facing wall. The floor was six large, polished flagstones across, each stone lovingly outlined in white. The bare walls too were whitewashed, as was the arched ceiling. Icons adorned the wooden screen that concealed the altar. In the middle of my solitary room stood a brown ceramic holder somewhat in the shape of a pillar, or a phallus, on which rested a pan full of sand. In the window alcove I found a box of candles, a box of matches. I did not see the candles until the sun was already making its way in at the window. I lit a candle and set it upright in the sand. Waiting there, sitting, pacing, I came to understand how Julie Magnuson must have felt on the morning of her delayed wedding.

What did we have to talk about, Billy Dorfendorf and I? Had I been a young man, a man in my prime, I would have seized him by the throat and strangled him.

I need not bother you with the details of our talk. He accused me of wanting, in my collector's need, to box up the very darkness that I lived in. I ignored his exaggerations. He said I would crate up lakes and beaches if I could find a way. Tell me how, I told him, and I'll make you a rich man. He said I wanted to put words themselves under lock and key and I said, mocking his unstoppable tongue, good enough, I'll buy that too, go on out and get me a collection. He accused me, in his maniacal, hoarse whispering, of trying to steal the face of God. He had simply lost control of his judgement as well as of his imagination. I told him I did not want to vomit in disgust inside a chapel.

The column of mules had resumed its motion toward the chapel door.

Henry Ketch, in the harbour below the cliff, hearing the sound of the mules' hooves on rocks and shards, in his greedy eagerness, without waiting for a signal, began the climb toward our rendezvous. I, in my distraction at Dorf's torrent of abuse, left Henry's wads of C-notes and their containing canvas bag on the double chair in the chapel. I bowed my way through the wonderfully low door with my former agent.

They moved almost reverentially, the seven mules, each bearing a burden of icons.

We stood together in the sunlight for a full minute, I would venture, Dorf and I, before anyone recognized who we must be. I was clinging to his arm; the sharp light only made my vision worse, and I feared stepping by accident over the cliff that had not so much as a sawhorse at its flat, sharp edge.

Dorf and I were standing arm in arm when Julie Magnuson and Maggie Wilder both at once recognized, if not me, at least their wedding dress.

One of them gave a shout. I am persuaded to this day it was Julie who shouted, and I am persuaded it was not a cry of surprise but rather a shouted command.

Dr Manuel De Medeiros, concealed in a kitchen in one of the small, square houses built against the outside wall of the village of Kastro, pulled the trigger.

The idea of motive is difficult, one might even say impossible, yet much of our so-called law hinges on just that impossibility. Who would presume to describe another's motive? Do we pretend to understand our own motives?

Manuel De Medeiros had no cause to hate me. He was, after all, living with my legal wife — my, if I might offer a correction, legally dead wife. And I suppose that too raises questions. Could Julie, being legally dead, make any legal claims to accumulated property or even to neatly counted and bundled one-hundred-dollar bills?

But that subtle question was not the question vexing poor Manny when he pulled the trigger on the rifle that was larger than he. Or at least it would have stood taller than he, had he stood it on its butt. But he was not standing the rifle on its butt, he was leaning it on a window ledge, pointing it, standing close behind it with an eye levelled behind the sights. And a black-market military rifle has, surely, more than adequate sights.

The sound of the shot on that quiet morning, following after the delicate clink of hooves on stone and the mournful but brief cry that was Julie's, came thunderous to our ears.

It was the sound of the shot I noticed first, not the consequence of the shot having been fired. Again, I could rely little on my failing eyes. That is, the event had already occurred when I heard its report.

But to get back to the question of motive. What was the role of Fish in all these events? If his motive was as pure as Maggie would have it, why is he now living at Deadman Spring with Julie Magnuson and the good doctor? Are we not to see in that arrangement Julie's compulsion to live with two men? But why would Fish go along with so unsatisfactory a relationship?

It was Fish who, on that earlier day when the other shot was fired, the first shot, insisted most vehemently that Manny De Medeiros had drowned. How then was he attached to the man who, fired upon in the past, was now so busy shooting in return? Or at least Manny had been busy shooting. Before he could pick himself up from the floor where the recoil landed him, other events were transpiring.

I am persuaded that Julie and Manny had arrived on the island of Siphnos with no other intention than blackmail and robbery. They did not, I am willing to grant, have any designs on my life; the shot fired by Manny was not intended for me.

Henry Ketch's head had made its appearance above the cliff's edge just as Manny fired his illegally acquired military rifle. Henry, instead of ducking down, as a wiser man might have done, stuck his head up over the rock ledge. He made great claims as to the veracity of his seeing. He claimed he saw me give a push to William Dorfendorf, there at the cliff's edge. I would insist that Dorf had steered me, a man legally blind, to the cliff's edge, and that he had done so with every intention of letting me in my blindness step over the cliff, into the rack of my own smashed bones.

Dear Henry was hardly to be trusted as a witness. Three years in a Greek prison will give him sufficient time to reconsider what he found and what he lost and what he saw and didn't see. He was, I believe, exactly what Greek justice judged him to be — a base and unprincipled if misguided thief. He was fortunate to get so light a sentence.

The shot that Manuel De Medeiros fired hit William Dorfendorf in his raised left ankle and smashed that vulnerable joint to smithereens.

In all fairness, one must say it is possible that Julie Magnuson cried out to stop Manny from firing the rifle. They had plotted and planned, that is obvious and certain; they had even bribed a local maker of silver necklaces and bracelets to let them use his studio for a few days, there on that cliff's edge facing into the sunrise. What Julie did not plan for was her emotion on catching sight of me, my life threatened.

She must have realized, seeing me there in front of the chapel, garbed in our wedding dress, that she still loved me. She must have cried out to interrupt the very scheme she had hatched with Manny.

The shot did not simply hit Dorf in the left ankle; it more or less severed the foot from the leg, leaving exposed a variety of splinters of naked and curiously white bone. He was, one is tempted to say, left with not a leg to stand on.

Poor Dorf. I will say categorically he had not come to the chapel proposing to murder me. The act of revenge, in any case, should surely have been mine, not his.

Maggie and Julie at once saw the consequence of the shot being fired. It was as if Dorf's left foot exploded off his leg and in the process gave the shattering sound that was in reality the sound from the rifle being fired.

While Dorf was standing on his remaining foot, I, old as I am, might easily have given him a fatal push. The absolute truth is, I did nothing of the sort. I reached to steady him. In my own stubborn way, I loved the man.

The local police arrived so quickly it seemed they might have been sitting over their morning coffee waiting for a shot to ring out. Siphnians, since ancient times, have not been trustful of strangers. Consider the history of an island once so rich in precious metals it maintained a treasury at Delphi.

I was wearing my wedding dress. The policemen of Siphnos have a profound respect for brides. Not one of them would come close to touching me.

They attended instead to the corpse below us on the rocks, and their respect for monks was more difficult to isolate than their respect for brides. There were a few jokes made about Papa B's garb. He had fallen straight down and landed on his head, somehow causing some of the bones of his neck to force his tongue out of his mouth. I take this on hearsay; I could not have brought myself to look. His strange hat had become a container of sorts, and for a while the corpse did not seem to bleed. Papa B was not, apparently, in the habit of wearing undergarments.

Ida and Josie took the news badly. It was Maggie who got on the phone. Telephone connections to Maggie are not an annoying necessity but rather a nervous system. She got Ida on the phone and Ida cried and asked incoherently who would care for the body. Somehow, gruff, choking on her tears, she got Josie onto the phone as well, so Josie might hear the news with her own ears. Josie too burst into tears of shameless grief; she tried to say something of the wedding dress, but, like Ida, was not able to speak a coherent phrase. When Maggie told me of their responses I closed my old eyes and asked her to be quiet.

The insinuation that I was in some way intent on killing William Dorfendorf is absurd. The one person I might have wanted dead was Manny De Medeiros. Billy Dorfendorf was as much the gull as I. He believed that he had been the cause of De Medeiros's death. I too had believed that Manny, if not my wife, was actually dead.

I had made an error in believing that Dorf knew my wife to be alive and well. For many reasons, I had always loved the man, Billy Billy, with his ridiculous name and his wish to resolve his doubled name down to one. Finding treasures was his talent. He wanted above all else to live with the integrity of goat cheese and barrelled wine and dark bread. It was, if I might say so, Julie Magnuson who destroyed him.

Manny De Medeiros was a scheming little devil. But I was intent on mercy, not mere justice, that bright morning. I explained to the police, through a variety of incompetent interpreters, that I had been intent on recovering the icons for their rightful owners, whoever they should prove to be, and damn the cost. We are told that artists tell true lies; I, there on the cliff's edge, spoke volumes. Henry Ketch was a two-bit chiseller who was after money.

Three years for the possession of stolen icons and attempts to smuggle them out of the country would seem to me a fair enough sentence. Granted, Greek jails are not exactly a picnic. Maggie feels that by our staying in Greece we can make arrangements for him to have better care, even if there is no point in trying to win an early release for him. His home university, it turns out, took offence at his asking for an extended leave of absence to spend time in the slammer, and thereupon terminated his contract.

Someone picked up the jock's canvas bag containing the unmarked bills, and then failed to report the gesture. I myself, if I were given to pointing a finger, would point at Karen Strike. She alone knew what was in the bag. She, my sources tell me, is off somewhere in Bulgaria or Yugoslavia or some such place, with the blessings of the CBC, making her documentary series about the portrayal of women saints in Byzantine icons.

I looked rather an ambiguous figure myself, since Henry Ketch testified that I had, through the agency of

Karen Strike, offered him a cool million for his stolen icons and had made arrangements to have them go by boat to Cyprus. The boat's captain, as well, turned out to be anything but a friend. I explained that Cyprus had its Greek population that would see me as a hero.

To my surprise, it was Karen and Julie who ganged up on me. There was a delay in getting the body up off the rocks and back onto the cliff; then, to make matters worse, just as the body made its appearance at the edge of the cliff, the sling either slipped or broke and poor Dorf was in for a second crash.

It was a terribly hot day. The human body, in extreme heat, does not long retain its freshness. That factor, combined with the second fall — and it was no one's fault — made Julie and Karen both a bit testy.

Karen, for all the bags and boxes she was lugging around, was nothing if not efficient. She wanted photographs of Dorf's, so to speak, second appearance, as he was hauled up over the edge of the cliff wearing, in addition to his usual garb, a considerable collection of thistles. That was too much for me. I decided I must duck into the cool of the chapel.

The precious icons had already been unloaded into the chapel for safekeeping until officials of various sorts arrived from Athens and Thessaloniki and from Mount Athos. While I was sheltering in the chapel, to rest my weary bones, to get out of the heat, I made a modest enough offer to the policeman in charge. I wanted nothing for myself, I simply wanted to catch a glimpse of the icon of the face of God.

The two muleteers were hanging around, and not simply because the police officer in charge would not let them leave. They had delivered the goods, as agreed, to the very spot where I was to conduct my examination; they were willing, still, to make the delivery down the cliff to the boat. That there were four armed policemen loafing on the attendant pleasure boat was none of their concern. They felt they should be paid for services provided. And they both had considerable headaches.

The policeman who watched over the icons inside the chapel could speak no English and could not understand that I wanted, whatever the cost, to get a glimpse of one and one only of the icons under his protection. I was compelled to ask the assistance of the muleteer who, during the transfer of the packages into the chapel, used a number of colloquial expressions that to his tongue were borrowed. The policeman saw that I was up to no mischief, so he and I quickly hit on an agreement and a price. The muleteers, though the second of them spoke not a word of English, insisted on a considerable cut.

My eyesight, of course, was a problem. How was I to single out the parcel that Dorf had been so eager to save?

I offered more bills to the policeman and the muleteers. Time was of the essence. I smacked my head going out through the chapel door to ask Julie and Karen if they would be kind enough to step inside and give me some assistance.

Julie Magnuson and I had not spoken to each other in four years, since it is generally recognized that conversations with the dead are difficult if not impossible.

"If I see you again in that dress, think of yourself as wearing it to your own funeral," Julie said. "Get that through your head."

That was all she had to say. She seemed to feel she had to lean right into my mouth to say it.

"I take that as a challenge," I replied.

Karen Strike, the idiot that she could be at times, snapped a picture of me and Julie standing face to face. "For the Calgary *Herald*," she said. "This will make the front page back home."

Those two women, turning away, carting along enough camera equipment to open a studio, almost knocked Maggie Wilder off her feet. She was busy and then some, there outside the chapel door trying to explain to a pair of identical policemen who had placed handcuffs on her husband's wrists and were about to march him off to a private place of his own that Henry Ketch was, at best, a nincompoop, at worst, a dupe of his own desires. He, all the while, was goddamning this and that, in a language that neither of the intent policemen understood.

18

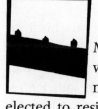

Maggie and I, consequent to our debates with the law and its minions, and recognizing that time is the great healer, have elected to reside for a while on our island home. And why, to begin with, would one want to leave paradise?

I had already rented a house that isn't quite a villa, and, along with it, a garden containing fig trees, olive trees, rows of beans and tomatoes, eggplants out the ears, cucumbers the length of your forearm, zucchinis, peppers red and green, a pine tree so huge it shades half the patio in the afternoon and provides us with pine nuts as well.

"We could start our own pizza place," Maggie suggested one day, giving way to that exciting laugh of hers.

The patio is blissfully sunny in the morning. I put on my dress. Maggie slips into a comfortable sweat suit, Adidas or some such brand.

I should also say we buried the corpse in a spanking new suit of clothes and underwear. It is the custom, here on the island, to disinter a corpse after three years and put the bones into a nearby chapel and let the church rent the emptied grave to another customer.

Maggie wants us to sit out the three years. We'll wait here. Papa B is seen as something of a saint by the monks and priests of Mount Athos. There is talk of building a chapel in his honour, on one of the many rock ledges that constitute Mount Athos. There have been inquiries about the possibility of moving his bones to the proposed site. For a price, I tell the astonished monks, jokingly.

Maggie and I, each morning, work for an hour or two on — dare we say? — a saint's life. It is a task we propose to have completed by the time Papa B's bones are disinterred and Henry is released from jail. I offer my recollections of events when she seems stuck for words. My failing eyesight remains a bit of a problem. Sometimes I ask her to read back to me what we have written.

I paid the piper and called the tune; I had my glimpse of the fourteen icons. Just a glimpse. That's all I was allowed. A huge icon of St George slaying the dragon. An icon that disappeared from Crete in the sixteenth century, something to do with the harrowing of hell. Messengers galore. Martyrs. A miracle or two. You name it. Those fifteen icons would have been the ultimate of my collections; I would have built for them a small secular chapel, somewhere across the lake from Deadman Spring.

Henry, unmitigated rascal that he was, had neglected to place the most infamous icon of all among the parcels that were to be delivered by mule to the boat that waited in the harbour. That it was delivered to this island cannot be doubted, since the culprits who brought the icons here and then went hightailing back to Thessaloniki confirmed in their discussions with the police that they had delivered fifteen parcels. Henry, on the night after his completion of a transaction with Karen, was as busy as a bee.

Sometimes in the late afternoon, after our siesta, after the heat of the day has been tempered by breezes from off the sea, Maggie and I go for a walk together. She slips into a clean sweat suit and sneakers. I drape one of my new shawls over the shoulders of my wedding dress. We had a local seamstress take in the bust just a tad. My dugs fill it out more than adequately, especially at those recurring times when I have a tendency to retain water.

We walk together through the cobbled or stone-paved streets of villages, along the neglected roads and mule trails and footpaths that connect village to village. We climb up to chapels on isolated peaks; we climb down to chapels in hidden coves. There are, on this perfect island, as I may have mentioned, four hundred and twenty-four chapels. We propose to visit each in turn, Maggie and I. Or sometimes we go back unexpectedly to one we have already looked into. Maggie gets the notion that she remembers our having seen the icon that I so want to see before it is too late; she suggests we go back and check. She leads me back.

Then we are not certain which chapel it was that she thought contained the missing icon, and so we start again.

We map our pleasant lives with visits. We have become objects of curiosity and praise on the island. Sometimes old men motion us to sit down to a glass of wine and a dish of olives. Old women cross themselves, then grope to talk in the language of gesture and smile and mime, inviting us to relax, to have a cup of Greek coffee, a plate of bread and calamari and feta. Tourists, of course, pesky things that they are, bring out their Kodaks. Sometimes groups of children run ahead of us, laughing, tossing bougainvillea petals or delicate stems of thyme and mint or the white of clematis or the bright vermilion blaze of pomegranate blooms or even dried mule dung into our path.

Some evenings we stay in our house that isn't quite a villa, Maggie and I, and sit in the shade on the patio and Maggie puts a beach towel over the shoulders of my wedding dress and tells me to close my eyes, which is hardly necessary, and she shaves me and does my hair.

"You must look the part," she tells me, often, while she is doing this.